Hamburger Haven

Hamburger Haven

a novel

Lindsey Martin-Bowen

Paladin Contemporaries * Scottsdale * Kansas City, Missouri

For information about permission to reproduce selections
from this book,
write to Paladin Contemporaries,
6117 E. Nisbet Road, Scottsdale, AZ 85254

Library of Congress Cataloging-in-Publication Data

Martin-Bowen, Lindsey.
Hamburger Haven: a novel / Lindsey Martin-Bowen. First
edition.

ISBN—13 978-1-881048-05-3
ISBN 1-881048-05-5
    1.   Domestic fiction. 2. Fast-food industry. 3. Child
    abuse. 4. Dysfunctional families.

Paladin Contemporaries, Kansas City, Missouri. Scottsdale,
Arizona

For Bob, for who knows what and who knows why—
love always

The author gratefully acknowledges Chris Baty and the NaNoWiMo for the inspiration, encouragement, and deadlines that helped her complete this novel.

She also thanks and acknowledges the *UMKC Law Review*, which published a section of this novel as "Caroline's Story," the narrative opening for her law review, *Words from a Teller of Tales: Can Storytelling Play an Effective Role in Feminist Jurisprudence?* in Volume 66, No.1 (Fall 1997).

Thanks to The Ecco Press for its 1973 edition of *Czeslaw Milosz Selected Poems (Revised)*. That edition contains Milosz's translation of "The Poor Poet."

Hamburger Haven

Chapter One
Haven West

Mick Buchannan inherited from his mother her pale blue eyes that seemed so innocent and pure. But he emulated his father, whose high-strung nature came from working as a policeman—first, a patrolman, then later a police sergeant. Mick's father released anxiety by pounding on a drum set while his step-mother played the organ. Mick's mother had died when he was eight, and he never truly bonded with his step-mother, who'd married his father only six months later.

Today, Mick wiped sweat off his neck and squinted again at the rising sun. It was one of those mid-west sunrises, where, above the clusters of overgrown, gnarled silhouettes of trees, the brilliant streaks of hot pink and gold overtook the sky. He squinted at the huge orange and blue Hamburger Haven sign outside. Much like a strobe light in a seventies disco, the neon sign glimmered more boldly than the colors in the dawn.

Up since four-thirty, he wasn't yet tired. It was one of those days that seemed to carry over from the night before, a night hazy with booze and sex and the woozy feeling from drinking too much too fast for too long. In fact, he hadn't been that messed up since he'd been in the Army Air Force. Yes, he'd been a good little soldier—spit and polish every reveille, Yes Sir, Yes Sir, You're absolutely right, Sir—but he'd get wasted not only during every leave, but also on every weekend for the three years he'd been stationed in Alaska. Last night, he'd let himself party too heavy in the vain hope that even with Independence Day coming tomorrow, the chilly air and the rain would send folks out-of-town, and it'd be slow this Friday. He realized now that was unlikely. Already, cars and trucks had been circling the Drive-Thru almost as incessantly as the choppers from

Vietnam, filled with guts and flesh shredded like raw hamburger, had whirled over the ice-capped mountains during his tours. At times, too, it seemed like the customers in those vehicles were as hostile as the enemy who'd shot at his buddies—guys who weren't as lucky as Mick. After a brief tour of Nam, he was stationed in the states, albeit in a frozen wilderness.

Suddenly, someone pounded on the front windows and caused the entire front of the building to tremble. Mick set down his coffee, stood and scrambled to the door. He unbolted it and leaned out. A tall, husky, unshaved man glared at him. He wore a huge jacket that made him look somewhat like the Michelin man. The wind whipped strands of the man's long, greasy black hair across his face, and he drew his arms to his sides and shivered.

Mick forced himself to display his full, managerial smile. "Drive-Thru's open. You can pull right in. And we open the lobby at seven," he said in a full-throated voice and blinked. He smiled again. "We'd love for you to come back then."

The man didn't smile. Instead, he wiped the back of his right hand on his left sleeve. "Carla here?" His voice was raspy, and he breathed heavily, his chest moving in and out as if it held pistons in an internal combustion engine.

Mick wondered who this unkempt man was. He knew Carla was a single parent, and he'd believed her ex-husband lived in the area. Maybe the guy was his shift manager's estranged husband. He forced another smile. "I'm not sure if she's on the schedule today." Hoping he could get the guy to relax, Mick forced a smile, this one tighter, less certain, once more.

The man cleared his throat. "Ya tell her Jonesy's here." Then, he wiped phlegm on the back of a hand he drew across his mouth. "And I gotta see her. Now." Jonesy's gravelly voice matched his demeanor. He crossed his arms and frowned.

Once more, Mick forced yet another grin. "I'll see what I can do." He closed the door quickly and watched Jonesy amble back to his black Ford pickup. Carla hadn't yet arrived, but Mick knew she was scheduled to show up in an hour. He hoped he could reach her at home. Maybe she'd want to avoid this character, who didn't seem all that happy to be here. By now, with this unlucky event, he was sure his day was going to be nuts. He desperately needed Carla to cover lunch. On the other hand, he didn't need some huge domestic fight in his front lobby. And Jonesy looked like the type who might have a pistol—or even an Uzi—stashed in his truck.

Mick hurried to his office, closed the door and locked it. Immediately, he picked up the phone, punched in Carla's line three times, let it ring and ring, but no one answered. He tried her cell. Still, no connection. He glanced back at the Ford pickup. Jonesy sat scowling and smoking a cigarette, from which he flicked ashes onto the parking lot. He seemed to listen to some music, too, because he tapped his fingers in time on the steering wheel. Nevertheless, he still scowled at the building. Mick didn't want to talk to the gruff man again. In fact, at times like these, he hated his job. He just wanted to go home. But he couldn't quit, not yet. Not with a wife, a step-son and step-daughter to clothe and feed. Plus, he had to send a bundle of his paychecks to his ex-wife. Even if Judith made a little money teaching and collected child support for his step-daughter, mainly they relied on his income. He'd brought her son Adam into the business, and that had helped some. But not enough. And sometimes Mick worried that Adam scared away customers with his goofy antics. Yes, generally, the boy worked hard, but he was so weird. He'd often go into a Buster Keeton or a Charley Chaplin routine when he was supposed to be swabbing the floor. And if he was at the front, he'd start talking like Groucho Marx. Mick usually kept him in the back doing prep and hoped he wouldn't have to fire the kid.

Smells of bacon and eggs wafted into the office. He picked up his pack of Salems, shook out one, lit it, and stomped back into the kitchen. There, José, a thin, muscular and very short Mexican, and Randy, a stout black man who usually hummed while he worked, hustled to prep the morning menu: Haven Tortilla-*Huevos*, Haven Hashers, and Eggs-Haven. Bacon sizzled and snapped on the grill, and Mick could see at least two trays of biscuits—or Haven-Hotties—ready to pop into the oven. "How's it going guys?" He glanced at his watch then back at the two crew members. "We've got twenty minutes."

José dabbed his forehead with a towel. "We on it, Boss." He grinned. "We doing fine."

But Randy shook his head. "I dunno." He leaned over the fryer and shook a bin of hash browns sizzling over the sputtering oil. "Depends on the crowd. We may be okay—but we may get behind awfully soon."

Mick glanced around and saw a line of breakfast sandwiches José was about to slip into the warmer. He shoved a loaf of bread back from the edge of the counter before a slice fell onto the floor. He smiled at his men. "Well, keep it up guys. Stay on top of it." He started to dart out toward the front, then stopped and turned toward the two crew members. "Anyone know anything about Carla's ex—what he looks like?"

"Yeah." José frowned then pursed his lips. "I think I saw him one time." He squinted. "Big, tough guy.

Smells funny, like loco weed." He pinched a thumb and forefinger together and drew it to his lips, then smiled.

Mick grabbed one of José's sleeves and tugged it. "Come with me."

After José confirmed that Jonesy was Carla's ex-, Mick tried phoning her again. Still no answer. He glanced back at the front parking lot. Jonesy puffed on a cigarette, and again, tapped his fingers on the steering wheel. Mick could see the truck vibrate from the bass sounds that pulsed from the cab. While he watched the intimidating man, Mick wished he were back in Mexico, Missouri, managing a safe little Haven store in the small, quiet town. Maybe the teenagers there might get a little rowdy now and then. But they didn't scare him. One phone call to a parent was the only weapon he'd needed.

Not so here. Even though this Haven was in a fairly safe suburb on the city's western side, in Kansas yet, Johnson County, with its reputation as a solid, middle-class suburb, sections of it equivalent to a Bullet Park of the Midwest, things could still go awry. Gangs of teenagers had terrorized Overland Park a couple of years ago. And he had no way of phoning their parents. This place was too big—no one knew everyone, not like in Mexico. Even if he could reach the parents, it probably wouldn't help. He doubted parents in the metro area exerted much control over their teens. Not that any parents living anywhere could exert that much control over their kids, not like Mick's dad had done to him and his brother. But that was a different time. And even if Mick wanted to be as tough as his dad, he wouldn't whip a kid the way his dad had whipped him. He squinted and drew another drag from his cigarette.

He watched Jonesy and wondered if he'd stir up trouble. Even if the guy didn't look all too happy, at least, now he didn't seem as ready to tumble as he had earlier when he'd pounded on the windows. Suddenly, Jonesy flung open a door and jumped onto the lot behind the sidewalk circling the restaurant. He glanced around the parking area and became so caught up in scanning the asphalt that he tripped on a clump of grass edging the lot before he stomped toward the building.

Mick watched Jonesy move toward the door, watched him take another drag from his cigarette, and watched him scowl when he'd lost his footing. Then Mick ran a quick review of his management class tips— Hamburger U, Intro to Charm 101. He also hoped he'd gauged this guy Jonesy's mood right, too. He slipped behind the counter, topped off his coffee, and poured another one into a Styrofoam cup.

Grabbing two packets of sugar and two creamers, he snapped a lid onto the cup and headed to the front door. He considered that he might be making a big mistake—Jonesy might have abused Carla. Or maybe he'd beat their kids and Carla was protecting them from him. Or maybe she didn't want him to know her whereabouts for other reasons. But Mick couldn't reach Carla now—and he'd given it his best shot. Besides, if he could make the guy feel a little welcome, it might relax him. Maybe this tiny act of kindness would help the family situation, too.

He set his coffee on a table, unbolted the door, and poked out his head. Staring at Jonesy, who now leaned against the entrance wall, Mick said, "Could you use some coffee?"

Jonesy blinked. He stared at Mick a long time, and then scratched his chin. Suddenly, he spoke. "Don't mind if I do, partner." He moved toward Mick.

Mick shoved the door open wider. "And hey—it isn't windy in here." He nodded toward the line of tables. "Have a seat."

Jonesy stared at him again, then slowly, he smiled. "I'd take ya up on the offer, but I need tah get to work. I was just stopping by tah tell Carla tah go by my place so we can figure out when I can pick up the kids. He glanced at the ground then back at Mick. "See, uh, I don't gotta phone. And I don't like tah use the one at work. She wanted me tah take the kids this weekend. I'm glad to do it. I miss those kids. But last night, I couldn't get by her place tah work everything out."

Mick grinned. "I know what you mean. I got an ex-wife and two kids in Columbia."

"So you know the drill." Jonesy grinned and threw back his head. "You get tah see them much?"

Mick handed him the coffee. "Not really." He shrugged. "Work too many hours. And it's a long drive."

"Too bad." Jonesy frowned and looked at his watch. "Can you pass the word on tah Carla? Thought she'd be here by now. And I can't be late."

"Sure thing, man. I'll let her know." Mick watched Jonesy amble back to his truck and drive off. He glanced at the clouds that again thickened into a green soup. Their color and gnarled shapes made him feel uneasy. Nonetheless, he hoped the rest of the day's problems would be solved as easily as he'd solved Jonesy's.

Chapter Two
Adam's Revenge

At a little after one, Adam came in for the evening shift. He wore his long black hair in a ponytail that he tucked under his Haven cap. Alternately morose and hyper, Adam wasn't tall—just a little more than five-foot-eight. But he had a commanding presence that made him appear well over six feet. He usually dressed in black, and perhaps his mastery of martial arts, especially Tae Kwon Do, made him appear larger—or to have the confidence of a larger person. The other crewmen, many of them older and larger, respected him, and generally, other men avoided teasing him or provoking him into a fight. On the other hand, Mick found Adam could sometimes act just stinking weird.

That afternoon, the kid brought a glass jar of flies into Mick's office. He stuck it on Mick's desk. Mick glared at the jar. About seven insects—all wingless— scaled the walls of the glass cage.

Adam grinned. "I caught all these in the lobby," he said. With both hands, he grabbed the jar and held it high above his head then placed it back on the desk. "I pulled off their wings. So now, they're walks—not flies." He tossed his head back in laughter. "What do you think?"

"Adam, I think you're nuts!" Mick tried to frown. Instead, he covered his mouth, which had begun to curl into a smile, and shook his head. "Why didn't you just swat them?"

Adam shrugged. "I guess I wanted to see if they could survive as 'walks' not flies." He turned to leave.

"Wait—" Mick looked down at the jar and noted that Adam had punched holes in the metal lid. He picked up the glass prison. "Take this outside and let these things go. I mean, way outside—far, far away from the entrance. Or you can just bury the jar somewhere. Just get it out of this restaurant. And go out the back—don't take it near the customers."

Great, Mick thought. *That'll put Judith in some wonderful mood.* Adam's return to live with them hadn't been part of the plan. Even though Mick had liked the kid, the sixteen-year-old had more than tried his patience—the boy had sent him over the edge. He started drinking more again, and when he was sober, he felt constantly on edge. Here, this kid was supposed to look up to him—but at home, Mick was no authority figure. He didn't want to be, either. No way did he want to become his father—a cop without a thread of mercy. So they muddled along, with Judith calling the shots about discipline, he yelling at Judith when he'd had more than he could take from the customers at the Haven and the kids at home. At times, he just wanted to run off, to disappear. But he didn't know where he'd go or what he'd do to survive.

Besides, most of the time, Judith was sweet. She was pretty and bright. She ran the household relatively smoothly, except when something angered her, and she could flourish and even save money on a tight budget. Plus, Mick loved her breasts and her butt. Maybe the situation wasn't perfect, but he knew it was better than most guys had, at least, those he knew. And the sex was great. He wished they could find a way to spend more time alone together—and he could find a way to spend more time away from the Haven.

After Adam left, Mick picked up a travel brochure someone had left in the office. Its cover pictured the rugged beige cliffs filled with the ancient pueblo ruins of New Mexico—somewhere near Taos or the Rio Grande. He flipped through the pages, which brought back many happy memories.

The summer after third grade, the summer after his mother had died from cancer, he and his older brother Dave had gone to Colorado and New Mexico with Uncle Todd and Aunt Madge. His uncle had driven a huge, beige and brown RV, and he'd towed his red Volkswagon beetle behind it, facing backwards so the trip didn't run up the car's mileage. His uncle was clever like that. After they'd set up base near some town or Indian reservation, they'd drive to groceries, tackle stores and tourist spots in the VW so Uncle Todd didn't need to maneuver the RV through narrow streets. Plus, he didn't need to fill it with gasoline except for the long excursions. But back then, the gasoline was cheaper than staying in motels. Mick smirked. He wondered if it would be today. Thumbing through the brochure, he pictured his uncle Todd, who'd laughed often, his belly shaking. The man had enjoyed playing jokes on Mick and Dave, too. One morning, the boys awoke suddenly with their hands in buckets of warm water. Another day, he'd sent them on the trail of a "dodo" bird, which Uncle Todd had sworn he'd spotted in the canyon. Of course, the boys never found the extinct bird. And later, their uncle explained why. Unlike Mick's dad, Uncle Todd knew how to show the boys a good time.

His uncle had also helped Mick's career. He owned and ran the largest Dale Carnegie franchise in the Midwest, and he had Mick take the course twice. So by the time he was twelve, Mick had learned how to make people like him—quickly. And today, all his employees loved him, they always did, no matter which franchise he worked for, no matter what job he held. Most of the time, Mick liked people, too. Until after he got lit. Then he resented them—and almost everything else about his life. Mainly, he resented not having the money to take trips like those he'd enjoyed for several years with his uncle, not having the money to buy the car he wanted, and not having the money to party as much as he wanted.

Suddenly, the office door flew open and startled him out of his reverie. "Boss Man, come look!" José yelled and waved for Mick to come to the front of the store, where a number of employees and a few customers gathered at a window. Mick hurried to join them. Out on the lawn, not far from the street, Adam was standing on his head and balancing the jar of wingless flies between his soles. Then, he'd kick the jar into the air and catch it between his feet, roll it a few times, then toss it again. He still wore the Haven's long, white apron, which folded back toward the group and nearly covered his face. Although Mick couldn't help grinning, he shook his head. He sighed, headed out the door, and stomped over to Adam.

"What in the he—are you doing?" Mick barked. "We don't pay you to be a clown. I mean, this isn't McDonalds. Besides, if you want to perform these stunts, you need to join a circus."

Slowly, Adam brought his feet forward; his soles still clutched the jar. He lowered it gently to the ground, then pressed his feet against it and sprang upright. His long hair was loose now and flapped around his face. "I timed out," he said. "This is my first break." He grinned, then pulled his hair back and wrapped a rubber band around it.

Mick shook his head again. "Can't you see how you're making me look?"

"You?"

"Yes. I'm the manager here. And you're my stepson. Everyone here knows that."

Adam shrugged and nodded toward the restaurant, where employees started clapping. "They all seemed to enjoy the show." He grinned.

"That's not the point."

"And your point is—

"Look, I like to have as much fun as anyone." Mick perched his fists on his waist. "But this is going too far—it's too crazy."

"Why?"

"For one thing, how many customers want someone preparing their food who has just rolled in the grass and played with flies?"

"They're walks."

Mick frowned.

"You asked me to swat them. And you know I can catch them better with my hands than with a fly-swatter. So if I swatted them, it'd be with my hands."

"Not in front of customers—"

"Okay." Adam sighed. "I get your point there." He shrugged. "I was just trying to liven up the place. It gets awfully routine, you know."

Mick inhaled deeply and pointed at the jar. "Stick that damned thing inside your car, and I don't to want see it again. I mean it. If I see it again, you're fired."

"The flies might smother in there."

"Good. They'll be dead by tomorrow anyway." Mick turned and marched back to the restaurant.

Adam shrugged again and followed him part of the way, then he turned toward the parking lot. But he slowed his gait to nod in three directions, as if he were bowing to a crowded stadium, and he flashed the peace sign at the employees who still gawked out the window. Then he grinned again. Broadly.

Chapter Three
Krystal's Tale: *The Golden Z*

Momma took me along when she bought decorations for her Mexican fiesta. Actually, the fiesta was my idea. Well, kinda. I was planning a party, too, and I didn't know whether I wanted a Hawaiian luau or a Mexico fiesta. Well, Momma grabbed onto that fiesta idea like a cat after a catnip ball. She wouldn't let go of it, either. So I knew I'd be doing a luau. I also figured a party might take her mind off my step dad Mick, so I helped her best I could.

"Get that one, too." I pointed to the donkey piñata with hot pink ears. Momma held a blue one under one of her arms. "We can put it in the dining room and hang the other in the kitchen."

"Or maybe over the deck." Momma smiled, picked up the donkey and stuffed it under her other arm. This was the first party Momma had planned in over five years, the first one since she married Mick. Most of her friends don't come around much since he moved in. I don't blame them. I don't like Mick, either. His breath smells like rotted bananas mixed with an aftershave that stinks like gasoline. Smoking one Salem after another and drinking beer after beer, he sits at the kitchen table and repeats almost everything he says. And every night, he scrunches his face till he looks like a donkey or maybe a mule with a mustache, belches a loud one, then laughs, as if it's funny. Sometimes he pounds on the table and cracks it and calls me or Momma "stupid" or "bitch" or even, "cunt."

I especially don't like how Mick treats Momma, yelling at her for nothing. Sometimes he hits her, even after she bought him a gold sports car, a 280Z. Zelda, he named it. And now, on evenings when he doesn't work, he drives around the neighborhood, his music booming,

"Every step you take" and "There's a little black spot on the sun today" over and over.

My sixteen-year-old brother Adam taped the cuts for him. Adam repeated the same songs about six times each, like Mick asked him to. I used to like those songs, but now I hate them, almost as much as I hate the way Momma's eyes droop at their corners now-a-days and the slow, sorrowful way Momma walks and talks anymore, that is, until she started talking about this party. I think she's happy 'cause her old boyfriend, Joe, a musician, is getting together a Mariachi band for this gig. I used to think Joe was a dork. But after living with Mick, I see Joe's okay. And it seems Joe stepping back into her life already began perking up Mama, like water does plants.

"Let's get streamers, too," Momma said, her eyes glimmering and happy-looking, "and balloons." She even smelled happier today—more like an iris than a rose.

"No, that's too much like a birthday." I crossed my arms. I liked her being happy, but we didn't need to look like dorks—or maybe some kind of nerds, but not the type who were computer gurus, just the weird kids who had no sense of coolness.

She saw my expression, frowned, and scanned the aisles. I thumbed through plastic bags of red, yellow, and blue blowouts. I pointed to some hot pink and turquoise Chinese lanterns that looked fiesta-like.

When we stepped outside, Momma lit a cigarette and exhaled a circle of smoke. "Let's go to Target. We'll find cheaper candy there." Momma always hunts for bargains, even for parties. She got Zelda for a deal, too, she says.

"Can I pick it?" I asked then grinned. I knew she'd let me. She always lets me pick candy for surprises for my cousins and for the special Christmas plates she gives to the neighbors. So we spent all afternoon buying supplies, and that evening, I sat on the deck by myself while Momma washed dishes. I felt happy and peaceful tonight because Mick worked late—till midnight. The thin wind felt good on my cheeks. I stared at the backyard, especially at the maple where the spirit lives now. I named the spirit Zebyn. Actually, I didn't name him—that was the name he sent to my mind. Sometimes I worry I'm crazy because most people don't see and hear spirits. Of course, most people don't have *The Gift*. Momma told me that when I was only three years old, psychics at a fair said I had *The Gift*. And Cindy and Sherry, the girls next door, have seen Zebyn. In fact, Sherry felt Zebyn push her to her knees. They described him as smoky-colored with burning green eyes, shiny like those green fluorescent ropes some restaurants give to kids. That's how I see him, too. So I figure I must be okay.

I was about go into the kitchen to help Momma with dishes when I heard the 280z's loud rumble and its stereo's loud blasts. "Every step you take, I'll be watching you," the car wailed. Apparently, Mick left work early. I was worried, too, 'cause I didn't know why. Mick manages a Hamburger Haven. He's the big boss there. Sometimes, it's okay when he gets off early 'cause someone just relieved him. But other times, he leaves 'cause he's mad at some customer. Then, he pops open his beers the minute he steps inside the house. He guzzles them fast and yells all evening, blames me and Momma for some customer mouthing off to him. Like it was our fault. Like we were even at The Haven. Anyway, that night I watched Mick closely. He backed the car under Zebyn's tree, like usual.

He says that way, it'll get shade. He didn't back up real fast so I figured he must not be mad. But I watched him to be sure. He stared straight ahead, stroked his chin, and frowned. That worried me. Maybe he'd had a run-in with a customer. Or maybe I'd left something in the yard. I tried to remember if I'd used any of his tools, but my mind didn't work too well 'cause I was so nervous. He glanced at the dash and flung open the door, stepped out and bent over to get something out of the backseat—his usual twelve-pack.

Then he tugged up his pants, closed the door slowly and glanced up. He smiled. That was good I figured, but I still wasn't sure. Finally, he lumbered on his wobbly, bowed legs across the yard all leisurely like. So I felt relieved.

"Hi, Mick," I cooed and smiled as if I were his friend, But his breath—this time smelling of charcoal and peppers—about choked me.

He grinned a starched smile, all stiff-like. "What are you up to, Little Miss?"

I hated him to call me that. He had no right. Still, I tried to make my words roll smooth as honey. "Watching the tree blow in the wind."

He squinted at me, then at the tree. "Ain't no wind today." He stopped at the railing and pulled out a pack of cigarettes.

"A little one's flickering."

"Ain't much." He shook the pack and tilted it toward me. I shook my head. Okay, so maybe I swipe a cig here or there. But what kinda man offers one to a twelve-year-old?

He pulled out a new black lighter. Childproof. "You seen my red lighter?"

"Me?" I tried to look innocent. "Why would I want it?"

He scowled. "Like you'd never use one?"

"I didn't say that." The wind stirred again. "There. Did you feel it?"

"Yeah. But ain't enough to make tree branches move." With that, he grabbed the twelve-pack and stomped into the kitchen.

I looked back at Zebyn's tree. Its branches twisted and fandango-ed with the breeze. I knew Mick had lied about the wind. But Momma says I'm precocious sometimes. I'm not sure what that means, but I think it's kinda like being smart aleck. Or maybe it means I see spirits. Spirits send messages to me, too.

And sometimes, that spirit Zebyn makes me do weird things, like carve on my skin. This summer, I etched a circle with a line through it on my ankle. Then, I rubbed ashes into it, the way Indians used to do. See, it wasn't that Zebyn actually told me to do this. It was like my hands couldn't obey my brain. Zebyn guided my hands—he just plumb took over. In fact, I don't remember cutting on my ankle at all. That evening, though, Zebyn had been quiet. Then, he jumped into Mick's Z.

"Get out!" I yelled at him. His green eyes just glowed brighter. I glared at him, crossed my arms, and went inside. Momma sat at the table, and Mick yakked on and on about his wonderful car. "Think I'll wax her tonight."

"Again?" Momma frowned and her shoulders slumped. Mick, see, waxed that car every two days.

"Yeah. Need to protect it from the sun. Keep my baby pretty."

He used to call Momma that, I thought, but I said nothing.

Momma sighed, and Mick stepped outside. I watched him while I helped with the dishes. Zebyn was behind the wheel now. He glowed when Mick rubbed on wax. And it was like Mick was in love with that car. He'd wax a section. Then, he'd polish it and stop, step back, pull out a cigarette, light it, and stare at his reflection in Zelda. He finished the hood, downed a third beer and slipped behind the wheel. He still didn't see Zebyn, who leaped out of the seat and now sat on the dash, glowing brighter than ever.

Mick cranked up the stereo and Zelda roared outta the drive.

"Where does he go after he waxes Zelda?" Momma sighed again. Her eyes and shoulders went all droopy. In fact, sunlight filtered in and high-lighted her blonde hair so she looked like a wilted, yellow mum.

"Just cruises the neighborhood." I made up my mind that there must be some way I could help Momma out of this mess. The fiesta might be the key.

Joe got the band together—but it was an ordinary band, not a Mariachi group. We weren't too disappointed 'cause we don't know any Mexicans in our neighborhood. Momma said he'd just been kidding. Besides, the guys agreed to wear sombreros and play, "Tequila Sunrise" and "Margaritaville." Momma mixed some Sangria with lemon and orange rinds floating on it, so during the second set, the guys substituted "Sangriaville" for "Margaritaville." Joe liked to do tricky things like that to make Momma laugh.

My friends and I thought the food and its smells were better than the music—Joe and his friends are just too much of a seventies' sound. But Momma cooked two huge pots of chili, tacos and burritos, and enchiladas— some with cheese, some with meat. All those tomato-y, spicy smells wafted through the kitchen window onto the deck and drive, where the band set up under the floodlight on the garage.

Things moved strangely that night, though. My boyfriend Jimmy showed up in a huge, turquoise sombrero and his dad's Old Spice cologne, and his shorts sagged so much, the rims hit below his knees. Momma and I laughed. My cousin Jenny flirted with Jimmy, and Jimmy slugged me. That made me figure I better dump Jimmy. So I slipped away and let my girlfriend Andrea handle them. She's taller than Mom and has lots of muscles. Meanwhile, I sneaked up to the deck's edge behind Momma and her girlfriend Gwen, a dark, pretty woman from Momma's undergraduate days, the days before she started taking school and life so seriously. I pretended to listen to the band, but I eavesdropped.

"Mick seems enthralled with the Z," Gwen said.

Momma nodded and forced a grin.

Gwen nudged her husband. "Reminds me of Michelle and the Mustang."

"You mean your daughter?" Momma knit her eyebrows.

"Yes. We bought her a Mustang for graduation, and she loved it. Waxed it every week, cruised around the city almost every night, spent hours fussing over it."

Momma squinted and watched her friend intently. "What happened?"

Gwen shrugged and wrapped an arm around Momma's shoulder. "She totaled it."

At first, Momma smiled, then she looked worried. But most the evening, her eyebrows weren't knit: she smiled and laughed. Even when she dashed around the kitchen preparing food, popped out to bring people plates and refills, she smiled. I noticed, too, that Joe watched her every time she stepped outside, even while he sang. Then, his stare would follow her after she returned to the kitchen. I noted that I'd mention this to Momma the next day. On the other hand, maybe I would wait until she was upset about something, like maybe something I did wrong.

Zebyn mainly bounced in his tree, but I saw him leap onto the roof behind the band. Then, he jumped into Zelda, parked under the tree again. And speaking of Zelda, wouldn't you know, Mick would try something to get everyone's attention. After the band finished at midnight, he turned up the Z's stereo full-blast, pulled the car into the drive, opened its doors, and left it—doors open, stereo wailing. I expected him to force everyone to their knees and pass a collection basket. My friends and I laughed at him, but we didn't let him see us. So I couldn't do much that night to help get Momma away from Mick. But I think she began to see what a fool she'd married. Of course, maybe Zebyn forced Mick to do that. In fact, Zebyn's power began to bother me. He'd started to control things more than I do. I especially got worried when Momma discovered my ankle a couple of days after the fiesta.

"It's a tattoo." I shrugged and tried to sound cool, like this was the only style to put on your ankles.

Momma grabbed my ankle and pulled it toward her, forcing me to sit. She ran a forefinger over the scar. "It looks like a zero with a line through it. It's the null set in Algebra." She looked at me with one of those stares that seems to bore right through your eyeballs. "Do you know what this means?"

I shrugged again.

"It's the sign for nothing. Zero. Is that what you think of yourself?"

So I told her about Zebyn, about how he controlled me sometimes, about how I couldn't remember doing these things. She didn't say anything. She knit her eyebrows, clenched her teeth, and got a wild, angry look in her eyes. I mean, dark green fires blazed where her irises had been. When her eyes went on fire like that, it scared me: It was as if some demon might hop out of her eyeballs.

Even though I told her about Joe's stares at the party, Momma didn't lighten up. In fact, she stayed awfully quiet the next week or so. She didn't seem sad, really, but awfully pensive. She started reading the Bible to me more often, too. One evening, just before dark, we sat on the front porch, and she read the part about King Saul having the Witch of Endor call Samuel's ghost from the netherworld. Samuel told Saul he'd die in his next battle. Even Adam seemed to enjoy the reading, and usually Adam hates to listen to Bible stories. A light wind blew against us, and we enjoyed the oddly cool July evening. Then suddenly, Cindy and Sherry's mom, Sheila, and the two girls scrambled across their lawn to our house.

"Judith, I need your help." Sheila plopped into the chair next to Momma and jabbered on. Cindy and Sherry sat beside me on the glider.

"Cindy can't sleep in her room anymore. She says she hears glass break at night." Sheila's eyes grew wide. She scratched her head, then crossed her arms and shivered. "And there's something off there. Something strange—I don't know—some strange presence."

"Maybe its Zebyn," Cindy said, and I glared at her. Sheila didn't know about him. So Momma explained about the spirit. Then she grabbed her Bible and headed next door. When we got there, I overheard Momma say something to Sheila about us girls having "wild imaginations." Just the same, we all held hands and prayed over Cindy's room. Momma clutched the Bible and spoke in tongues. Then, we moved to Sherry's room and did the same. It's a funny thing, too: usually Adam would've made fun of us. He didn't. But he said he could only see traces of energy—probably from the girls—no spirits. Next, Momma and Sheila went to attack Zebyn back in the tree.

"You girls must point him out to me," Momma said, "because I can't see anything."

I told her where he sat. Then, I pointed him out when he jumped from limb to limb. Momma swung her Bible at each spot I showed her. I couldn't see how this would scare Zebyn at all. In fact, I was starting to get scared. What if this angered Zebyn? What would he do for revenge? What would he have me do next? And I worried he might do something to Momma. She had enough problems already. Then, Adam offered to buy each of us girls candy at QuikTrip.

"I'm not sure we should leave," I said.

"No—let's go," Cindy and Sherry rang out. "We're scared." Such wimps.

"But what about our Moms?" I glanced back at the mothers. They ambled toward us. They seemed okay with the idea, but still, I worried.

"Momma's stronger than you think," Adam said. "She's a powerful fighter."

But living with Mick had weakened her, I was sure. "What're you going to do?" I asked her. I couldn't figure out what plan she designed that she couldn't share with me.

"Just go along with Adam," she said, then she and Sheila walked us to the edge of the drive, where they stopped and turned around. They moved back toward the tree.

Adam pushed me toward the sidewalk. "They'll be okay."

I stared at Momma.

She glanced back. Swooping her hands, she said, "Go on," and frowned.

So we left her and Sheila to handle Zebyn. I doubted they'd be able to do much, and I worried Zebyn would do something awful to them. I'd read about spirits making people go crazy—and forcing people to harm themselves. Kill themselves.

It's a funny thing, though, a short while after we strolled toward the store, I felt relieved. It was that light-hearted way you feel after heavy thunder-heads pour out their water, then break up and blow away. It was a fresh feeling like that, and a relieved feeling like you get once you go to the bathroom after you've waited a long, long time. I couldn't figure out where the feeling came from, so I just enjoyed it. And I also enjoyed talking Adam into buying us ice cream bars instead of cheap candy.

When we approached our house, though, the worry returned. Momma and Sheila stood at the edge of the drive. Momma looked pale, ashen. Pearls of sweat ran from her temples, down sunken cheeks, and dripped off her jaw. Her widened eyes focused on something distant. She rubbed her upper arms and trembled. Sheila also stared across the street and shook her head.

I worried that something terrible had happened. I worried that maybe our mothers had lost their minds. But, at least, both of them were intact—even if they looked dazed.

When we stepped into the drive, Momma looked at me, wrapped an arm around one of my shoulders, and drew me into a hug. "It's gone, now. You were right. It was something—an entity. I saw him when we walked back to the tree. But he didn't look dark. He looked like a cloud."

"What'd you do?"

"Like I said, he looked like a cloud—or mist—hanging over the fence back there. So I wasn't sure if it wasn't just the way lights hit the branches that made me see something. Then, Sheila and I stood under the tree. Sheila claims she enters the spirit-world through her sense of smell. And she said something smelled funny. So we prayed, and I exorcised him—or whatever evil spirits there were—in the name of Jesus, the way the Bible says. Then, all of a sudden, I felt someone—or some thing—shove my shoulder as if he were pushing his way through a crowd. I felt fingers—extremely cold fingers—run across my shoulders. Of course, I turned and stared at it, and I saw the ball of white mist I'd seen on the fence shoot out across the street. When I glanced at Sheila, I saw her gaze follow the same entity mine had."

"Whew!" Sheila interrupted. "It was a ball of light—like a fireball. And it shot out so fast."

"Did he go into a house?" I asked.

"No. He shot through the fence between the two houses, about ninety miles an hour. I still can't believe it." Momma stepped back and rubbed her upper arms again. "I'd never believe it if I hadn't felt it. The wind was blowing slightly, but this was different. It was no wind. Those cold, invisible fingers pressed into me like no wind could."

"Told you." I smiled. "When will you start believing me?"

You'd think that would've ended the craziness, but no. Although exorcising Zebyn calmed down our household somewhat, Mick was still crazy around that Z. Then, a couple of months after Zebyn left, after school had started and the air was comfortable so you couldn't blame people's daffiness on the clammy heat, Mick called home from The Haven. Momma's face held no expression while she held the receiver. After she hung up, she sighed, but I thought I saw a faint glimmer of a smile at the corners of her lips. "Someone wrecked into the Z."

"Was it Mick's fault?"

"He wasn't in it. He opened at 7:30 this morning, and he'd parked in The Haven's lot. Some teenage girl plowed into it. The car's ruined."

"Wow." I turned away so she wouldn't see me grin.

"I knew it'd happen. I just prayed he wouldn't be in it. Then, no one would give him a breathalyzer test."

You can imagine how Mick ranted about this the next few weeks, claimed someone must've cursed him. And it was weird: Zelda was the only car in the lot, and the lot was four car-rows wide. Me, I wonder if Zebyn didn't control that girl's car. Or maybe Zebyn flew to The Haven and hung out there. The Haven's west of us, and that's the direction Momma pointed to on the night she exorcized him. At least, the insurance company totaled the car and paid Momma its full price. Mick drives the Escort now. Plus, Momma's been humming songs around the house again. Joe started playing in lots of coffee shops. He sends Momma flyers about his gigs and phones and begs her to come. I'm encouraging her to go and take me along.

Chapter Four
Judith's Safe Harbor

At least nine persons pressed their fingers on Mick's back, his arms and his head. Judith smelled their heavy, incense-like cologne, not Patchouli, but someone definitely wore Jasmine scents. One woman pressed her palms on Mick's neck and with fiery eyes that seemed to shoot lasers, she stared at Judith. All of the others closed their eyes, lifted their chins, and prayed in tongues, their voices growing louder, tones varying— some dropping to bass, others lifting to high A's. At least four of the prayer warriors were men, a few more were women, and Judith was surprised how much their ages varied: some were barely into their twenties, others at least in their seventies. One woman wore a prim, pink pantsuit with a button-down, floral blouse, much like an outfit her mother would wear. A young girl wore a handkerchief skirt, another dressed somewhat like a Goth. The men's attire and countenances varied, too. One old man wore a bandana, while a young man wore a suit. And yet, they focused their energy into one strong, current. Judith felt heat emanate then rise from their hands and engulf them as if it were a cloud, except this heat was dry, not quite like a sauna, but more like the heat emanating from an oven. She felt it engulf her, too, then penetrate her chest and suddenly, she felt so relieved, so much at peace, more at peace than she'd felt since she'd first returned to the Midwest.

She, too, joined them in speaking of tongues. The syllables flew from her lips and created phrases that sounded Hebrew, Greek, with a word here and there that sounded French. She marveled at how those tongues were always there—always waiting to spill from her tongue. Her Catholic mother had always been skeptical of this phenomenon.

"How do you do it?" she'd snap whenever a conversation between them drifted into discussing glossolalia. "And how do you know what you're saying?"

"It's the language of God, Mother. I don't always know—but I sense what the words mean. And they just come. They're always there. Like right now. *Cumadeah, eh cumshey Diea kiya monde de vie.*"

"Well, I wouldn't want to say words I didn't understand." Her mother sighed. "You might be saying something evil."

"I break it up with praising Jesus, Mom. Just to make sure I say the right things."

"Then why bother with it?"

"It's the language of God, Mom. It's prayer. And after I let those words come out, I feel so much better, so much more connected with God. In fact, too often, I get caught up in the world and neglect the tongues. But when I remember to let them come, I'm so much more at peace. And I don't swear then, either."

"Well, at least, that part of it is good."

"It's all good, Mom."

And tonight, the sounds of the tongues surrounding her and Mick and spewing now from her mouth, released the existential weight she bore on the back of her neck, too. She cried, and the hot tears rolling down her cheeks felt like a liquid salve. She felt happy, too—full of joy—especially now that Mick was finally aligning himself with God. He'd quit chiding her for her beliefs, and now they could unite against the world's wiles. And finally, he'd quit—or, at least, cut back—on drinking. She prayed that wasn't too much to hope for.

Then suddenly, she felt an even more intense sense of relief. She believed everything would be okay, now, whatever happened. Whether Mick quit drinking or not, something had changed. She felt it change in her chest. And her life, her children's lives, would be safe. They would survive. In fact, somehow, they would do more than survive—they would flourish.

She opened her eyes. Although the persons still prayed, the sounds grew softer now, and one or two of the prayer warriors withdrew their hands, even though they continued praying.

Then suddenly, Marguerite, the large, white-haired woman who led the tiny congregation of merely thirty persons wrapped her arms around Mick and Judith. "I sense also a spirit of alcohol and a spirit of nicotine hovering around Mick. We've got to shake it off—scare it away." Marguerite stopped and inhaled deeply then went into speaking tongues. Then she shouted, "We command it to leave now, in the name of Jesus!" and shook her fists above her head. Then she opened her eyes, brought her hands down to her sides and stared at Mick. "You must fight against these demons, too. They're strong ones. You have the Holy Spirit to help you now, but you must also battle them by refusing to let them return to you."

Teary-eyed now, Mick looked at her and nodded. Judith smiled. She felt happy this evening. Perhaps now Mick would quit drinking—they could be a real family at last. She hoped his conversion was real.

Chapter Five
The War Comes Closer

Mick worried about his marriage. Even though he'd made another deal with God, the way he had when he was sixteen, when he'd promised to quit drinking if his dad would return the maroon Valiant he'd confiscated from Mick after he'd found a six-pack in the back seat. Still, even though he'd stopped through the weekend after his "healing," Mick couldn't give up his habit of downing a twelve-pack every night after work. Judith no longer seemed patient about this. Before, she'd said little about his drinking. It seemed she didn't notice it much. But now, she'd ask what "number" he held in his fist, and she no longer sat with him in front of the television to watch DVDs of *Rocky,* all twelve of them. So now, as if it weren't enough to struggle every day at the Haven, it seemed he'd lost his standing at home. Then, after the events with the 280-Z, Judith grew really distant. She didn't seem to share her thoughts with him any more. Once, she'd read poems she'd written and had asked for his input. She acted as if his responses meant something. But she hadn't done that for months, maybe a year now. And she no longer acted interested in romance. Little by little, she'd closed herself away from him, and he wasn't exactly sure why. Even if now he sensed that the beer had a little to do with it, he wondered why it hadn't been more of a problem before, or, at least, why he hadn't understood that. Maybe he was just becoming more aware of things.

He leaned back in his chair and lit another Salem, then exhaled loudly. At least, he thought, Judith smoked, so she couldn't rail at him for that. On the other hand, she didn't smoke anywhere near the two-packs-a-day he did. And lately, she demanded that they smoke only in the kitchen, the basement, or outside. So no more puffing in the living room. He didn't mind that so much because he spent so much time in the basement where he used his new circle-saw to cut boards and build a wardrobe, then small tables. But certainly, it was weird that Judith had started making these rules about stuff that had never seemed to bother her until lately. They'd been married for six years—why change anything now? He couldn't figure out women, he never could.

"Mick! Hey, Mick!" Adam's words rang outside Mick's office. "Come quickly! You gotta see this—now!"

Mick stubbed out his cigarette. "Oh, God, what now?" he griped aloud, then yanked open the door and slipped around the corner to the front line. There, he found Nancy, his newest employee, pouring a tossed salad from its neat, plastic box into a Haven bag. She handed it to a customer, a middle-age woman. The customer's mouth gaped.

"Hold on, M'am," Mick said, grabbed another salad from the cooler below, and put it on the counter. He smiled. "Sorry 'bout that. This is her first day." He grabbed a bag and placed the boxed salad into it. "What dressing did you want? In fact, I'll give you as many as you want—on the house." He smiled broadly.

The woman brightened and took her bag.

Mick shook his head and glared at Adam. "Nancy gives a whole new meaning to 'tossed salad.' Take over the register. Have Nancy do prep until after lunch."

God, Mick thought. *Some of the pretty ones were so stupid. Who'd fill-in another spot at the front?* he wondered. It seemed no one wanted to work lunch hours except these daffy ones who were hard to train.

He returned to his office and flipped through applications. Most of them were a couple of months old. Generally, they'd hired applicants on the spot. So those left in the slush pile weren't the best candidates for the jobs here. That's how Nancy slipped into her position at the front, a crucial spot.

Shortly after this event, a young man showed up in Mick's office. With his cropped hair and erect military-like posture, he reminded Mick of himself during his youth. Only this kid was tall—at least six foot two—and stout, not fat but muscular. He looked like he

could play as a tackle, guard or lineman for the Kansas
City Chiefs, or maybe work as a bodyguard for the Mafia.

"My name's Rod, Sir," he said and reached for
Mick's hand. Rod's direct eye contact impressed Mick.
"I've just come back from Iraq, and I'm in college now,
JCCC. And I won't lie to you about staying here forever.
I've joined the Reserves. But I know I won't be shipped
back to Iraq for at least a year. I'd sure like to work for
your company while I'm going to college. I won't use my
schoolwork for an excuse, either. I'll work as hard as any
of your full-time folks, even if I don't get any sleep." Rod
grinned.

Scratching his chin, Mick looked Rod over. He,
too, was a fine-looking soldier. "Are you available during
lunch hours, say from eleven until two?"

"Yes Sir." Rod's reply was so prompt Mick
expected a salute and a click of the heels to follow it.

Mick smiled. "You know, I believe we just had an
opening pop up today. How soon can you start?"

"Tomorrow's fine, Sir." Rod smiled and nodded.
Mick half-expected him to salute, but he didn't.

Chapter Six
Willy

Exhausted at two a.m., Judith lay on the couch and thumbed through the most recent issue of *The New Yorker*, the magazine she'd read every day when she'd still held dreams of acting on Broadway. Tonight, she read about the war between Orson Welles and Sir Laurence Olivier, and how, when they vied for the role of "most amazing actor" in the Bard's retinue, they shoved each other off a Strafford stage. It fascinated Judith. Her acting teacher had performed with Olivier or "Larry," and Judith felt a kinship with Willy S. As a child she'd hide, after curfew, reading his plays with a flashlight, as she did with the tome *My Wicked Ways* by Errol Flynn,

a writer, too, though more renown for his movie roles
and dates with teens. She'd started reading Willy when
she was eleven. First, she'd read *King Lear*, the play that
enraptured Orson. *And that seemed fit, with his bass
voice, bushy eyebrows and heavy Heathcliff looks*, she
considered. Later, she read *MacBeth*, but didn't like
Lady MacBeth. In fact, although she liked the action in
these plays, she didn't like the messy deaths, not like the
kid in *Shakespeare in Love*—John Webster. Tom
Stoppard wrote the young lad who liked blood and rats
into the film. Judith found that ironic: The real John
Webster wrote morbid plays in Willy's wake, and few
others than Elizabethan scholars would know who he
was, right? Had not Daniel Webster revived the Bard a
century later and compiled explanations of English
definitions, sounds and idioms, few persons today would
note that surname at all. Thanks to Stoppard, today,
"going to Webster" now held multiple meanings. Yes,
Stoppard liked to chase quibbles as much as Willy did.

  The *New Yorker* feature claimed the rivalry
between the two actors flared up after World War II, in

April '46, when Olivier and the Old Vic Company hit the Apple. There, Larry swatted bees to upstage Sir Ralph Richardson's Flagstaff. At the same time, Orson directed an elephant in "Around the World in Eighty Days": a few critics scoffed at his "forty-five tons of sets" that they named "Kane's warehouse." And Orson linked Hamlet to roller skates.

As a child, Judith had watched Orson on TV and shivered at his deep-set eyes and scowling face. She'd believed Sir Olivier was above all-that—a dignified Shakespearean actor, no less, who only later stepped into Hollywood. But here, Claudia Roth Pierpont averred that when old Larry wanted to fight, he grew as devious and nasty as Kane. In fact, he got away with shenanigans as much as Hemingway did, but unlike the author, he didn't seem to care if anyone heard about it.

For after Orson played on TV with Lucy, then suffered bad luck and finally had hopes for "Chimes at Midnight" on a Dublin stage, Larry asked him to direct "Rhinoceros." This was not the encouragement it first appeared to be. In fact, Claudia wrote, by 1960, Larry's stature had skyrocketed, and he could have brought the play, "Chimes" to London. Instead, offstage he portrayed a hard-core villain who harmed Welles. Such irony.

Larry claimed Orson flubbed up as a director, shooed him off the stage, directed the play himself, and went on to win rave after rave. Then Olivier worked with a voice coach to lower his tones to a bass, and he snatched Orson's role of the Magic Moor. But afterwards, Larry's "Othello" met his doom, with one critic comparing him to "Sammy Davis, Jr." So Karma sprang up again, till finally, the American Welles ended, dying at age 70 in '85 from a heart attack during sleep. There, he had lain with a typewriter on his belly while he was adapting "Julius Caesar" to video. He'd planned to film *Lear* again, too. And YouTube still shows scenes of his movies today. Or so *The New Yorker* said.

Judith wasn't sure about that—she hadn't checked out YouTube. In fact, she spent so much time online answering e-mails from students that she rarely enjoyed the Internet anymore. At times, she used it to research trivia—and historical background to create handouts and tests. But it was no longer the same as her honeymoon days on the Net when each surfing session was an adventure. It had morphed into another form of a phone—no longer magical. Nonetheless, she enjoyed the *New Yorker* feature, which confirmed her credo: She'd found most men to be inherently evil and selfish.

Suddenly, Judith heard noises upstairs. At first, it was a swishing sound, then something thudded onto the floor just above the living-room ceiling. She watched the vibration a second then sprang from the couch, her long hair and nightgown flying, leapt steps two at a time, and maneuvered down the hallway to Krystal's room.

After she shoved open the door, she scanned the messy bedroom, with shorts, jeans, T-shirts, and shoes intertwined in a lump on the floor, papers and books forming uneven stacks on her daughter's desk and dresser, and here and there, wadded Tootsie Roll wrappers clustered in corners like bees around a hive. Judith shook her head and then spotted Krystal swaddled in sheets beside the bed. With strawberry-blonde curls framing her face, the girl breathed heavily, almost in snores. Apparently, she'd rolled over and tumbled to the floor again. This had happened every three days or so the past few weeks, although it'd rarely happened before then—not since Krystal was about four years old and thrashed so much in her sleep. Tonight, Judith debated whether to lift her and place her back in the bed or let her sleep on the floor. If she picked up the child, she might wake her. Besides, the evening was warm so she wouldn't be chilled. Okay, perhaps she wasn't the best mother, but she'd leave Krystal there once she checked to ensure the sheets were loose enough to allow her to move without cutting off her circulation.

She ran her fingers through her daughter's silky hair, squatted, and kissed one of her pink cheeks. Then, Judith smiled. Even if her twelve-year-old was no longer the innocent second-grader that she'd treasured, she still loved this wily creature, this sassy creature who'd become defiant, and yet, like her son, made her laugh when the rest of the world created tears. She kissed her once more, stared another few seconds, and then went back downstairs.

Chapter Seven
Adam Walks

Adam moved the mouse around the pad to form a design he hoped to sell to Internet customers. Using Adobe Acrobat, he'd create designs for stationery or T-shirts, anything someone wanted, and he'd create any logo someone ordered for any business. It wasn't the same as the etchings he'd drawn in community college, but if he got lucky, he could earn a living doing this, he was sure. He didn't want to spend the rest of his youth sweating at the Haven.

Finally, he figured a walk would inspire his creativity. The September evening was perfect—a soft wind rubbed his cheeks and rippled his hair. He liked the way the light changed in the fall—from gold to silver—and the faint scent of dry leaves seeping into the air. This evening, the sun had just dropped below the horizon, and the red skies reflected its gold streaks. Evenings like this made Adam happy to be alive. He inhaled deeply as he lumbered along.

After rounding a three-block square in the neighborhood where their house stood two blocks west of Wornall Road, he decided to hike east, to the other side of the abandoned trolley tracks. He'd once dated Sheila, a girl who lived in Armour Hills, a pleasant, old neighborhood not far from there.

Just as he crossed Main Street, kitty-cornered, to head north on the east side, from the corner of his eyes, he saw a black SUV speed through the intersection. "Idiot driver," he muttered and scurried across the street. The truck slowed down and started pacing alongside him. He worried that maybe the driver heard him. Even if he had a black belt in Tae Kwon Do, he didn't want any trouble. So he looked the other way and walked faster. He could hear the truck staying beside him, though, and he became more worried. Figuring he could zigzag to Shelly's house and the truck would likely continue north on Main, he turned left at 70th Terrace and headed east on the sidewalk.

The truck turned, too. Adam picked up his pace again and hoped the driver would turn into a driveway. Certainly, the guy wasn't planning to stop and pick a fight because of the few words he'd said under his breath. Of course, it could be he hadn't heard him at all. Perhaps he was just some thug looking for a fight. He knew some guys out there had heard of his prowess with martial arts and wanted to spar with him. But Adam wasn't interested. He'd learned martial arts for defense. He wasn't that large, so he figured he'd use his mind and agility to protect himself.

The light was thinning now, going deeper into twilight. Soon it'd be dark, and maybe the guy would stop the truck and try to urge into a battle. Adam walked even faster.

The driver honked his horn. *Okay*, Adam thought, *I'll turn around.* Perhaps it was someone he knew, even if he didn't recognize the truck. "Adam!" the driver shouted in a low, thick voice. Adam turned toward him. It was Joe, his mother's old boyfriend, the musician who'd encouraged him to get into music. He hadn't seen him since the party his mother had thrown two years before, when Adam was sixteen. Joe's hair was white now, and Adam wouldn't have recognized him, except for his voice.

"Hey, kid, you need a ride?"

Adam stared at him a long time. Finally, he nodded and moved toward the door.

Chapter Eight
Judith Reminisces

Judith sat at her computer and wrote a handout for her students. *Wacky Ways to Warm-up*, she named it. It went like this:

Wacky Ways to Warm-up

Open a book, any book. Dictionaries work best. Close your eyes, then point to a page. Open your eyes. You must start writing by using whatever word to which you pointed. If you pointed to an article, such as "an," "the," or "a, "start your sentence with the word following it. Use this focused free-writing exercise just after you wake in the morning (or whenever you rise). It worked wonders for Hemingway. It can for you, too.

Sit at a computer or by your journal with pen in hand. Write a poem. This need not be a prizewinner, but just do your best. You might begin by describing the sunlight filtering through Venetian blinds or the ominous clouds churning over your concrete patio. Play with the poem's language for about fifteen minutes, then embark upon your writing project.

Flip through a magazine until you find a provocative photograph. Imagine you're one of the persons in the photo. What are you saying? Thinking? Feeling? Why? Who are you talking to? Write about what's on your mind as if you were the character in the photo for about fifteen minutes, then start your project.

Jaunt (or if you must, *drive*) to an enclosed shopping center (or try an outdoor mall, such as the Country Club Plaza, if the weather permits). Find an outdoor café that serves whatever beverage you prefer. Open your journal and describe your environs.

Then ***watch the people*** around you. Describe

their physiques, clothing, and movements. Capture their voices and words. Then begin your project.

And, of course, **dream**. Jot down your dreams in your journal. Respond to them when you first begin your "writing time." Then start your project.

Suddenly, after she typed the last paragraph, she recalled the dream she'd had the previous night. Her ex-boyfriend Joe was in it. So was Natalie, his former live-in lover. Even though the dream's images had grown hazy, she remembered the three of them in a bedroom. It seemed as if he were trying to convince the women to join him in a *ménage à trois*, but she wasn't certain if that had happened at all. She merely remembered the image of the two of them sitting on a bed and she'd stared at them from the doorway. Joe had leaned back and pulled his knees toward his chest. Like a rooster's comb, his black, spiked hair splayed across the pillow case. He'd smiled his cocky smile, his eyes glittered madly, and he'd tilted his head to the left.

Sitting across from him in a chair, Natalie said nothing, but tugged her fingers through her mousy-brown hair. To Judith, Natalie's face resembled a faded dishrag, wrung out and hung to dry. Nearly fifty, Natalie hadn't matured much, except physically. Her jowls sagged, and she continuously squinted as if she shielded her thoughts. Actually, Judith hadn't minded that Natalie lived with Joe. She'd moved in with him not long after Judith and Mick married and moved to Mexico. No, it wasn't merely Natalie living with Joe that irritated Judith. It was the way Natalie had acted so proud that she and Joe were together—and then, when they broke up—the way Natalie had blamed Judith.

And indeed, she had blamed her. In fact, the last time Judith had seen Natalie had been at a meeting designed to shoo Judith from Joe's life. One Sunday evening, Natalie had phoned Judith and had asked her to meet at a local Denny's for coffee. When Judith arrived, there Natalie sat in a booth. The scarf she'd wrapped around the crown of her head didn't camouflage her greasy, stringy hair, and the bags under her eyes seemed puffier. She wore a large, white, button-down man's shirt with its tail poking out from under a red pullover sweater. *Perhaps she'd attempted to sport a "grunge" look,* Judith thought but said nothing about the attire.

"Hello." Natalie's smile was nearly a sneer. She fumbled with her lighter, lit a cigarette and exhaled a long stream of smoke. "I've ordered a pot of coffee. We can share it."

"Sure." Judith slid into the booth, picked up a menu, and thumbed through it. Nothing seemed enticing. "Whassup?" Although she still didn't feel comfortable using the phrase, she said it anyway. She figured it might loosen up Natalie, who seemed to prefer hip language. But Judith didn't watch Natalie's face for a reaction. Instead, she focused on the menu and reasoned that if she ordered eggs, the protein might steady her nerves. On the other hand, she wasn't sure about that choice. In fact, when she later glimpsed at Natalie, who now fidgeted and puffed madly on a cigarette, Judith started to lose her appetite.

Natalie cleared her throat. "Joe has been cheating on me. I'm sure of it. I thought the affair he'd had last fall was over, but I'm not sure."

Judith no longer felt hungry. She looked back at the woman who now frowned. "He's been very apologetic, but I'm not sure it's worth staying with him. Plus, I need to learn more about what's going on."

"And you asked me here because—?"

Natalie sipped coffee then squinted. "Because you're so obsessed with him. I just wanted you to realize that if I leave him—which I may do shortly—it would be silly for you to pursue him."

"Obsessed?" Judith couldn't believe what Natalie had said. Even if she might still be attracted to Joe, certainly, she wasn't obsessed with him. She felt like slapping Natalie. Instead, she shook her head. "If I were obsessed with him—that was years ago. Remember that portrait I painted of him?"

Natalie nodded.

"That was my 'good-bye' gift. I gave to him because I knew it was over—and I've had no intention of getting together with him since then." Judith poured cream into her coffee and focused upon the rivulets of Half-and-Half blending into the dark brown liquid. She marveled at the irony of Natalie's words. Since she'd married Mick, she'd had no interest in Joe, except as musician, whose work she admired. Plus, Joe freelanced as a proofreader. Judith had hired him to help her on a magazine she edited, and she'd done her best to maintain a strictly professional relationship.

But Joe had done otherwise, beginning just after he and his band partner had performed at the Mexican fiesta. Then, when they'd met to exchange copy, he'd embraced her—and often tried to kiss her. Although she'd allowed him to kiss her lips a few times, mainly to appease him so they wouldn't battle and she'd lose an excellent proofreader, she'd maintained her distance, at least, emotionally. And physically, they'd done no more than youths did at parties in junior high. In fact, the way Joe would often write her brief notes or phone her and talk about sensual—even sexual aspects—of her looks, it appeared if anyone were obsessed, it was him. Not her.

And now, she had to put up with Natalie's accusations?

"Joe says that you wear extra perfume when you drop off copy to him," Natalie continued. "He says he lights incense to get rid of the strong smell." Then she sniffed. "But you don't always do that. Now, for instance—it doesn't smell strong."

Judith stared at her. Indeed, Natalie's face resembled a dishrag, tonight even more than usual. Although Judith watched her pennies when buying anything else, her perfume was expensive—*Trèsor*—not some cheap dime-store stuff that left behind stenches of wilted gardenias. She'd hoped this wouldn't happen, but she felt defensive. Even after reminding herself that she wouldn't let her ego control her, she felt burning inside her chest.

"I mean, look at you—you're an attractive woman," Natalie rattled on. "You don't need to go chasing after some guy. After all, we're almost fifty."

Judith wanted to say, *speak for yourself.* At age forty-three, she didn't yet connect with the half-century decade. Instead, she squinted at the woman, who was four years her senior, and said nothing. *Projection*, she thought.

Then Natalie chided her for taking Krystal with her to Joe's gigs, and went on and on about her "chasing" Joe. Finally, Judith could take no more of it.

"Actually, Joe's the one who's wanted to get together," she said. "And I have written proof."

Natalie grew quiet. "Really?"

"Yes." Judith inhaled deeply. She hadn't wanted to betray Joe. On the other hand, he'd been coming onto her, as if he'd fallen in love with her again. Simultaneously, he was betraying Natalie with some third woman. *Joe deserved it*, she decided, then sighed. "He's written me some notes." She sipped her coffee.

Natalie wanted to see one of the notes—then decided she didn't need to. Then she changed her mind again and wanted to see it. So she followed Judith to her house, where, with Natalie trailing, she raced upstairs and dug from one of her files the first note Joe had written the summer before, where he admitted he was still attracted to her physically. Natalie's hands shook when she held the note and appeared to re-read it at least three times. She frowned and water started to rim her eyes.

"I'm sorry." Judith sighed again and embraced Natalie. "He's a jerk. You're right—you're better off without him."

Although Judith felt sorry for Natalie, she had to admit, she felt a certain sense of pleasure in seeing her in pain. At any other time she wouldn't have felt that way. But Natalie's words about Judith being obsessed and her criticism of Judith's mothering skills had stung her. Still, she'd been kind. She hadn't divulged how Joe had admitted that he'd asked Natalie to move in only after Judith had married Mick and moved to Mexico, Missouri, and how he confided that he'd realized he'd made a mistake in less than a month afterwards. She hadn't divulged how Joe kept phoning her and trying to seduce her—putting his arms around her and drawing her to his chest, kissing one of her cheeks, then her neck, and finally, after her resistance had melted some, her lips, or how they'd lain and kissed on his Oriental carpet. Nevertheless, Judith knew she'd had the last word. She'd won. And she hadn't spoken to, heard of, or seen Natalie since that horrid day they met in the restaurant.

At least, not until in her dream, two years later. She wondered then what had become of Natalie, who left Joe the week after she'd seen his note. Joe had phoned Judith then and screamed at her.

"You should never have done that," he'd railed. "Natalie's gone ballistic. She pulled out clothes I'd bought her and cut them to shreds. I'm worried about her. She might do something drastic. She gets crazy sometimes. See, she could harm herself—and it's your fault!"

"My fault?" Again, Judith couldn't believe the irony. "Like you did nothing?"

"But I didn't tell her anything. She's gone nuts now, hearing about us! You caused her to lose it."

"Really?" Judith inhaled then spit out words like bullets. "I think your affair with that other woman caused her to lose it more than anything I did."

Joe said nothing for awhile. "It was more than an affair." He paused for a few more minutes. "In fact, we're getting back together." Then his voice grew loud again. "But you better not say a word to Natalie, or you'll be sorry. I'll lose any respect I have left for you!"

"And when will I see Natalie?" she'd quipped, growing bored with the insane conversation. "It isn't like I'd seek her out."

So even though Joe and his partner fulfilled their commitment by performing at a celebration party she'd held the following summer, he quit proofreading for the magazine, per his new lover's request. And after he married that lover, for a long while, he performed in no gigs. Then, when he did, Judith never went to one of them. In fact, she hadn't spoken to him since. For the most part, she hadn't seen him, either, except one night when she'd stopped at a neighborhood grocery store. In fact, once, when she'd come back to her car, an old Saab 900, she spotted him getting into his truck, which was parked near her car. She stared at him a long time, and he looked at her. Neither of them said anything or even nodded. She had noticed, however, that he had dyed his white hair to a dull black—and she wondered if he hadn't also undergone a face lift, perhaps, she thought, to be more attractive to his new wife several years younger than him.

Yes, such a dream—it brought back uneasy memories. Now, recalling those scenes made her nauseous. She was relieved that neither Joe nor Natalie peopled her life any longer. And now, only once in a while did she miss attending Joe's gigs—and it happened only when she heard acoustic guitars blending in harmonies that created watery sounds that seemed to flow through her. But when she recalled the outcome of the twisted friendship with Joe, the longing quickly left. It was, more than anything, the music she missed, not the neurotic womanizer who performed it.

She sighed once more, stared at the monitor a moment, and saved the exercise in the file folder she'd set up for composition classes. The back door slammed, and she pushed away from the computer, rushed downstairs, and saw Adam come into the kitchen.

"Whassup?" She asked and smiled.

"You won't believe who I ran into." He grinned and moved his eyebrows in a Groucho Marx imitation. Adam's eyebrows were naturally thick, like his father's.

"Who?"

"Well, I was going to Shelly's, and as I walked north on Main, I heard a truck that seemed to pace itself with me. Like when I'd walk faster, so would it. When I slowed down, it did, too. So I thought someone was trying to give me trouble. Then I looked over, and guess what?"

"Who was it?"

"It was Joe."

Judith felt queasy. "Really? Did he stop and chat?" She tried to keep her face expressionless.

"Yeah." Adam grinned. "He's usually friendly to me. He's performing again. In fact, he said he'd like me to come by and record his new group."

"So are you?"

"I dunno." Adam shrugged. "I might. But you know, I've often wondered just how serious Joe is about performing. Sometimes, I think he just played the guitar to get women."

Judith grinned. "You may be right. He quit playing after he got married." She shrugged. "And I've heard that he's moved back into his old house."

"Really? From whom?"

"Joe's old buddy Charlie. He says Joe's wife kept calling the cops—that those two got into some awful fights—real knock-downs."

Judith shrugged and smiled. "Guess it's good we didn't make it as a couple. I wouldn't want any police scenes here."

"Right." Adam smiled and opened the refrigerator door. "A bit more excitement that we need. Speaking of which, who drank my Coke?"

Chapter Nine
Mick Reminisces

Sometimes Mick thought about Mary, the former general manager who'd left about three years ago to become a regional manager. When he worked under her, he'd often wondered if maybe Mary was coming onto him. It wasn't merely that she was almost always kind, but most times, it seemed her eyes would light when he arrived at work. And she'd been behind each promotion he'd received and she'd requested raises for him several times. Finally, she'd urged the corporate office to put him into her position when she'd left. He remembered the day she'd given notice and recommended him to be her replacement. She'd acted so distant. All day, she'd sat in the office, unusual for her, and she'd said little. Usually, she'd greet him with a huge smile. But that morning, she'd barely nodded when he walked in—and she hadn't smiled, either.

"Anything wrong?" Mick had asked.

Mary shook her head.

"Was everything prepped okay?"

Without looking up from the thick stack of papers she clutched, she nodded.

"You're just busy, huh?"

She seemed to bite her tongue. Then she looked at him and appeared to force a smile. "A little." She shrugged. "Talk to you later."

So Mick wondered what was up. He'd hoped the store wasn't going to be inspected again. Even though they'd passed each health inspection, he often worried that some day they wouldn't. If the health department closed them down, that meant no paycheck. Okay, he figured, if something was up, Mary will tell him about it. He smiled at his boss, hung up his jacket, washed his hands in back, then went up front. Only a couple of folks were at the counter, and one of them waited for an order. The other, a mid-aged woman with a small boy— three, maybe four years old—beside her pointed out menu items to the child. Mick pulled out a toy puppet of a hamburger sandwich with eyes on the buns and a huge wide, mouth where the hamburger lie. It also had arms and legs that flopped in front of the sack where Mick's arm had slipped inside.

"Hello Little Fella," Mick said in a high-pitched, screechy voice similar to Alvin the Chipmunk's. He moved the puppet's arms and turned it side to side in front of the boy. "What's your name?"

At first, the boy squealed. Mick was unsure if he'd frightened the kid, but then he giggled and grabbed toward the puppet. "No, no, no. You can't eat me. You have to eat a little hamburger. I'm too big."

"Look—Nana!" The child pointed to the puppet. "The ham-ga-bur talks!"

The woman smiled and patted the puppet on the head. "Put an extra fry with that order," Mick said to the clerk at the register. "On the house."

The woman looked at him and beamed. Mick felt good then. He liked for customers to respond. It made his job seem worthwhile. It made his life seem worthwhile, at least for a few minutes.

Mick grabbed a cloth and headed to the lobby. All the crew members were busy, so he'd bus the tables, especially when Mary was in such a strange mood. He stopped for a minute and stared out the window at the gray clouds churning. For a few seconds, he felt as if he were back in the Mexico Haven, where he first started with the company just before he and Judith got back together and married.

Actually, back then, they'd reunited after a twenty-year absence. They first dated the summer after his freshman year in college. However, they'd known each other since both of them were seven years old. Judith's family, consisting of seven children, had moved across the street from his the year before his mother had died. It had been a God-send, really, having her four brothers to join him and his brother Dave in sandlot-football skirmishes and to hunt sparrows in the open

country at the end of their street, where still a few farms
fended off the encroaching developments. Plus, hanging
around with her brothers gave Dave fewer opportunities
to pound on Mick. Although he'd always liked Judith
and thought she was pretty, he didn't become close to
her until the end of high school. Then, he'd fallen in love
with her, but the situation was hopeless. Neither his
father nor his step-mother wanted him to date her
because they feared he'd get her pregnant. And his
father was close friends with Judith's father. So the two
of them would meet at movie theaters or discos. Then,
they'd leave either Judith's car or his and spend the
evening together.

After a few months, though, Judith became
disenchanted with the situation. He remembered the
night they broke up. He never let on how much it killed
something inside him to hear her words.

She'd drawn her fingers through her long hair.
"Look. I need someone that I can be with publicly."
Then, she'd frowned. "This is ridiculous. Either you tell
your step-mother that you're going to see me, or that's it.

We're not seeing each other again. We won't talk to each other again. In fact, I won't wave at you when I see you drive by."

Soon afterwards, he'd left to live with his uncle in Illinois. But he'd partied too hard there, and his grades had plummeted. So he enlisted in the Army Air Force. He'd learn to fly, experience adventures, and he fully expected to be sent to the front lines. After boot camp, during his first leave while he awaited his orders, he'd returned to Kansas City and stayed with his parents. And he saw Judith. They'd gone out "publically," as she'd formerly requested, in his Valiant. By then, he was popping "white crosses," and offered her some.

She'd frowned and shook her head. "No—not speed. I might smoke some pot here and there—but that stuff's dangerous."

He'd shrugged. "It keeps me going."

She'd stared at him a long time but said nothing. They saw a vintage film, *Catch-22*, but Mick couldn't take it. Riddled with soldiers and whores dying, and a crazy main character Yosarian, entrapped in an absurd world he wanted to exit, the movie reflected Mick's life in the army. At first he said nothing—he didn't want to spoil the evening for Judith. But, then, she'd seen the film the week before. They left at intermission.

"Sorry you didn't like it," she'd said. "It was so cool, so *surreal*. It kept me interested every minute."

"It wasn't that." Mick rubbed his nose. "I just can't handle it now—not tonight. Too heavy."

"Actually, the book's humorous, not as eerie as the movie. The book had me in stitches, but I can see why the movie upset you." She'd smiled, and the moonlight lit her features. Yes, the moonlight—mainly, he remembered the moonlight and the warm seventy-degree day in October. That image with Judith all aglow in its center, he'd carried with him for months—years, actually. And she had smelled so sweet—like lilacs or gardenias, some spring flowers. Her scent mixed with the smells of early autumn—oak and maple logs burning in fireplaces, winter mums—had kept him going during the months of his first tour in Viet Nam and later, when he was stationed in Alaska. That night, the moonlight hit her high cheekbones and transformed her into an Indian. At least, she looked like an Indian to Mick.

He hadn't visualized her that way before then. That night while they stood chattering in the moonlight, he'd wrapped an arm around her and drew her to his chest.

"Listen," he'd whispered. "I don't want you to go and get married on me." She lifted her head and stared at him. "Is this a proposal?"

"Yeah. I guess so. I mean, I think you and I will get married."

"Oh? So we're engaged?"

"Well, I don't want us to be tied down."

She'd frowned. "So you're not making a commitment or anything?"

"I mean, with me being away and all. And with you being in school. I want you to still have a good time."

When he'd returned eighteen months later, Mick stopped by her parents' home. They still lived across the street from his parents. Judith was married. She and her new husband, Frank, were visiting, and Judith had introduced Mick to him. He wore a heavy black mustache, and his shaggy hair hit over his ears. Later that afternoon, Judith's brothers, Mick and Frank played football. Mick tackled Frank and cracked his ankle. He later wondered if he hadn't broken it on purpose.

But after he left, on a train to Alaska, where he remained stationed during his tour in the service, he met a woman—or a girl, really—only seventeen, a cute blonde whom he married. They had a child, a boy, whom Mick rarely saw. So as part of the divorce agreement, she requested that Mick allow her second husband to adopt the boy, Mikey. With child support payments being so hard to manage on the army's low pay, Mick signed the agreement. He regretted it later, but he didn't know what else to do at the time. Besides, she'd hired some high-priced Chicago lawyer, so he knew he wouldn't have much say about the contract anyway. He couldn't afford a lawyer, and the army wasn't offering him one. So he just gave in—he hadn't seen Mikey much anyway. He figured the kid wouldn't miss him. And maybe it'd be better for Mikey not to know his biological father. After all, he'd become a screw-up, or so his dad had told him. So he shoved Mikey into that part of his mind where he stacked unsettling situations, such as his dead mother, Judith, and everything he lost and couldn't regain. It never surfaced again, either, until he was loaded.

By the time he left the service, he'd begun shooting speed and cocaine. Then, after being discharged in San Diego with little cash and no job possibilities, he became a runner for a drug lord. Fifty pounds of cocaine had been packed in the doors of the red Camaro he was to drive to Boston. But the dealer hadn't told him that two hit men would be on his tail to collect a debt the drug lord owed their mob boss. Mick figured something was up, though, when two men in a black BMW kept tailing him, even when he exited Interstate 15 into San Marcos and drove on a boulevard, then meandered through back streets. The men stayed far enough behind him that he couldn't see their faces. Mick figured he needed to swing back onto the freeway and stay in the middle of traffic. He wasn't sure what he'd do when the cars thinned out as he headed east.

They'd overtake him then, he was sure. Once back on I-15, he tried flooring it, but the men in the BMW kept pace with him. Although he first considered the men might be narcs, he later dismissed the idea. They'd followed him across California and into Nevada, past the Vegas exit. They would've stopped him by now—unless they thought he'd lead them to a big fish— and that fish would've likely been in Vegas, not somewhere farther east. Mick knew the top lord was back on the west coast. These guys weren't narcs—and Mick couldn't fathom who they were or what they wanted. He figured they knew about the coke hidden in the car because they kept pacing him, waiting, steadily waiting, it seemed, for him to be alone on the freeway.

Then, they'd attack him, he knew they would. He also figured that once they passed Mesquite near the Arizona border, the traffic would pan out, and the long stretch of desert highway would give them the chance to overtake him. The drug lord had paid him $2,000 in advance—the other half he'd receive upon delivery.

Okay, he figured, he'd have to give up that bonus. He stopped at a gas station and asked for an empty gallon container.

"Mighty dangerous carrying that in your car in this heat," the attendant said. "You sure you want to take this?"

"Got to," Mick said, and spread a twenty on the counter. "Got to get it to a buddy who's stuck on the highway."

The man blinked and said. "Awwh, none of these used cans are worth that much."

"Take it." Mick grabbed the can and headed out to the pump. He filled it halfway and stuck it on the floor of the passenger's side, then he swerved out of the drive and down the highway so he'd get a lead on the idiots following him.

From summer travels with his uncle, he remembered a canyon in Arizona that seemed to be close to the freeway. He tried to remember exactly where it was when he crossed the state line. He'd been right—the traffic had panned out. But now, this would be to his advantage. He floored the accelerator. He had to get there with enough time to get away before the BMW arrived. He glanced at the side mirrors and then in the rear-view one. He didn't see the car. He checked repeatedly as he accelerated. For a second, it seemed it appeared on the horizon. But he hit the gas, and shot ahead until he saw nothing behind.

When he arrived at the area he remembered, he swerved off the highway toward the cliff, leaving as much rubber as possible. Then he stopped about five feet from the edge of the bluff. Leaving the keys in the ignition, he tossed his backpack out of the Camaro, opened the gasoline can and doused the car's interior. He put the car into neutral and shoved it toward the edge of the bluff overlooking the canyon. He opened the driver's door and set the front seat on fire. Then he tossed the match to the back seat and slammed the door shut. He got behind the car and shoved as hard as he could. Slowly, steadily, the burning car rolled till finally, it rumbled over the edge, then flew into the canyon. He glanced around. The black BMW hadn't arrived yet, but he had to move fast. He ran toward brush about fifty feet away. While he ran, he heard the explosion when the car hit below, and huge streams of smoke rose and floated over the cliff. He'd hoped it'd be streaming still when the men arrived, and he waited, watching for them. He had to see which direction they went when they discovered the crashed car. He'd definitely travel the opposite way and change his clothes before he did.

So when he appeared, long-haired, unshaven and high at his father's house, the ol' man made him dry out on the couch in the living room. Mick quit everything—cold turkey—and suffered night sweats and shook until all the drugs left his system. He tried working for Judith's dad for a while, but he quit. Then, he'd hitched a ride to Mexico, Missouri, where he married again, had two kids, divorced, and came back to Kansas City to find Judith. Last month, it had been seven years ago since they'd gotten back together. And for the most part, he'd been as happy as he'd ever been—until lately.

Even finding Judith had been lucky. He couldn't find her name in the phone directory, but he looked her up under her father's name. Judith's mother readily gave Mick her phone number. So he'd called and made plans to see each other. Even though Judith hadn't expected him to arrive with all of his belongings in the bed of his truck, she greeted him warmly. And even though he hadn't expected Judith to look even an hour older than he'd seen her twenty years before and was terribly disappointed that she did—her cheeks gaunt, jaws angular, he greeted her warmly, too. After staying at her place a week, he proposed. Surprisingly, she'd said, "yes," and they'd been together since then. And usually, Mick was glad of it, even if sometimes, their fights drove him crazy.

"Mick—Mary wants to see you in her office— now!" The shift manager, Ben, shook Mick from his reverie.

"Right there!" He replied, wiped the table, and dropped off the rag in the sink on his way to the office. Mary sat calmly at her desk, but now, she smiled. "Sit down." She stood and pulled out the chair he'd sat in earlier that morning. She picked up her coffee mug and sat back in her desk. Suddenly, her perfume—a light, spring scent, like lilac, smelled stronger and she ran her fingers through the hair on the nape of her neck. Then she smiled again.

"What's happening?"

"I just talked with Dan."

"It's good you're still smiling." Dan was the Midwest manager for all the restaurants stretching from the Canadian border to Mexico, as far west as Colorado and as far east as Indiana. Usually, when Mary had talked with him it meant something was wrong. Apparently, not today. Mick couldn't help but smile back, with relief mainly.

"You're looking at the new manager for the five-state region, starting next month—or at least, starting as soon as I can make arrangements."

"Hey, congrats!" Mick felt happy for her and shook her hand. "So will they let you do that from Kansas City?"

Mary shook her head. "That's the downside. I have to sell my house and move to Illinois." She shrugged. "So do you and Judith want to buy my Overland Park place?"

"I'll ask. I know she's been wanting to return to Kansas."

"It's a ways, west, though." Mary chewed on her lower lip. "Still, you two might take a look at it. But that isn't why I called you in here." She smiled again. "I've recommended that they make you general manager here."

"Really? Hey, thanks."

"And you'll get a substantial raise—at least ten grand more a year."

Mick grinned broadly now. This was the best news he'd received in a while. He cuffed her left shoulder. "Maybe we could afford to buy your house." That, he thought, might cheer up Judith. She'd acted depressed because she thought their house was too small. She'd complained that she could never keep it from looking messy. "Not enough room to store accessories for four people," she'd argued. And she'd complained about the amount of money he spent on booze. "We could have a nicer house—more money in the bank," she'd gone on, "if you'd just cut back on drinking." Maybe, Mick thought, if he bought her a dream house, she'd let up. Then he could party as much as he liked. And maybe, just maybe, she'd share a drink with him once in a while, like she did in the old days, like she did when they were young.

Chapter Ten
Krystal Gives up the American Girl

"Why are you watching *Oprah*?" Momma asked and then stood in front of the screen. She clutched a cup in a dishtowel. She'd been drying it when she'd stepped into the living room. I figured she'd come in to ask me to help with the dishes.

"Hey, Mom, don't." I couldn't believe she'd done that. "Hannah Montana's on today."

"Really?" She stepped back and plopped onto the couch. "Miley Cyrus. That's Billy Ray Cyrus's daughter. You know, "Achy Breaky Heart"?

"Yeah. But she sings better."

"I like 'The Best of Both Worlds,'" Momma said and still clutching the dishtowel, watched the show. Her eyes glimmered.

After Oprah interviewed Hannah or Miley, she talked to her dad, Billy Ray, too. And then, Hannah performed for a hundred girls who'd waited in the studio. Then, Oprah took us behind the scenes in the American Girl Doll Hospital in Chicago. Some doll showed up there because a girl's brother scribbled all over the doll's face with permanent marker. I'd kill Adam if he did that. Of course, the girl probably had a kid brother. I'm glad I don't. And then, the American Girl Doll woman revealed next year's doll. She has red hair, like mine, and her name's Mia. She's a skater and her brothers are hockey players. I hope Momma will buy me one when they come out in January. Maybe I'll tell her I only want money for Christmas, so I can buy Mia the next month.

After we watched Hannah and finished the dishes, we packed into Momma's Saturn to go to the community college where she teaches and hit a

Christmas party. There were lotsa snacks there—chocolate candy Santas and balls, every sugar cookie you could think of with glittery sparkles on them, and there was real food, too—tiny quiches and itsy barbecued sausages. It was wonderful. But later, on the way home, after I ate all that good food, I worried that maybe we'd died and gone to Heaven, especially when Momma's car ran away with us. We had stopped at a light, and Momma pressed the accelerator to pass the huge, silver SUV next to us, so she could see ahead.

Then, the Saturn wouldn't slow down. Well, Momma got real worried. "Help me get this plastic mat up," she yelled while she tugged on the mat at the same time she down-shifted and braked. "Maybe it's pressing on the accelerator."

I pulled it onto my lap. She tried tugging at the carpet mat that had been underneath the plastic one. Momma, see, always has two sets of mats up front, just in case someone wears muddy shoes. "Oh no! It won't move!" She kept one hand on the steering wheel, and she kept trying to downshift, and the RPMs on the dash went wild. "Look for a shoulder—so we can stop!" she yelled, her eyes all crazy and bulgy looking.

There wasn't much of a shoulder where we were. All along the road, less than a foot of pavement edged the highway. No wide shoulders beamed in the distance, either. Instead, a narrow bridge ahead had nothing but concrete railings. And in the oncoming lane, a huge semi sped from the other direction. I started to get scared. But I didn't tell Momma that 'cause she didn't seem exactly calm herself. In fact, she seemed shakier than I was feeling. Her eyes looked wild, like they belonged on some palomino about to break away from his rider. I mean, it seemed her eyes had grown five inches larger in diameter. Her forehead wrinkled, while her mouth stayed agape. And she kept talking in a loud voice.

"This is crazy!" she yelled. "Braking barely slows this down—downshifting will probably cause the engine to explode."

We zoomed along, and I put my hands behind my head and bent over, pressing my forehead to the seat. I was so afraid we'd crash into something—another car, a tree, whatever. I started sweating, too. Even if it was November, it was about seventy degrees and the mean, old glob of a sun shined through the windshield and heated things up. Or maybe I sweated 'cause I was so scared. Momma seemed to keep the Saturn on the road and in our lane okay, which was amazing, 'cause she simultaneously tried to move the carpet away from the pedals, steer, brake, and stare ahead at the highway. Still, that car didn't slow down, and I wondered how we'd get outta this one. I prayed. I told God that the American Girl doll wasn't nearly as important as us coming out of this mess *alive*. And when I pictured all the evil things I'd done to Mick and sometimes, to Adam, I told God I was sorry again and again. I promised to be nicer. I promised not to make fun of Momma's fashion sense, either.

Then, just past the bridge, Momma spotted a shoulder, so she steered toward it and turned off the ignition. It worked. The car slowed down quickly, and somehow Momma swerved it onto the shoulder. Then, Momma was shaking. But she still pulled up the carpet and tugged on the accelerator. "It's no use," she said. "It won't catch. It just flops—there's no tension. Something's wrong."

She opened her door slightly. "Gosh, we're close to the highway." So she turned the ignition back on. I ducked back into my crash position till I was almost under the seat. The car revved up high again, but this time, it didn't take off, and somehow, Momma managed to maneuver the car farther away from the road. Then she turned off the ignition. She sighed and so did I. Finally, I tugged the end of my shirt tail to wipe the sweat off my neck and forehead.

Still quivering, Momma called AAA on her cell phone and talked to someone. "I'm sorry if I sound a little shaky," she said. "I don't know if you've ever been in a car you couldn't stop, but—I just have." It turned out, the AAA woman who'd answered had her accelerator do that, too. But she'd run two lights and crashed, Momma told me. So the woman put our situation on "high priority."

She musta, too, 'cause sure enough, in just a few

minutes, a tow truck came and put the car all the way on the bed. I was sorta surprised that it didn't just tow it behind like always. But then, I figured 'cause Momma told them what happened, the towing man probably thought he'd better not take any chances with that Saturn trying to run away again.

It wasn't until the next day that Momma's mechanic explained what happened. The O-ring in the oil cap had dried out. So the cap vibrated off and lodged itself on the cable leading to the accelerator. We couldn't figure out if we were unlucky because this weird thing happened—or lucky because we weren't hurt. The car wasn't damaged, either. In fact, Momma asked the mechanic if all her downshifting and braking had hurt her clutch, the brakes or the engine. The mechanic said the car has something in it that kept the high RPMs from hurting the engine. They'd checked out everything, he said, and all was fine. Plus, the whole thing didn't end up putting us in the Poorhouse, as Momma often imagined car repairs would do. It only cost Momma $22—$12 dollars for the tow and $10 for the new cap. But I'm not sure how many years the scary ride took off her life—and mine. And the entire event made me come clean with God. I agree to quit snickering at the toupee on Father Darey when it slipped off center during Mass. Plus, I promised to be more honest during confession.

But I also decided I'd begin taking action that very night. I decided right then that at least every month or so, I was going to nag Adam and Mick to check the gas cap, just to make sure that stupid "O-ring" didn't dry up again.

Chapter Eleven
Judith Rescues Jenny

Even if the wild car ride had frazzled her for the rest of the evening, at least, gazing at Hannah Montana on *Oprah* had cheered her up. Along with being shaken by an unruly auto, she became more upset when she watched TV later the night. Then, she caught *Frontline*'s reports about Darfur, where 200,000 died in the genocide and two and a half million more were forced from their homes. Mia Farrow and other celebs called the upcoming Olympics games in China the "Genocide Olympics," and a TV spokesmen deemed the situation required "a political process—political action." *So why, Judith wondered, did the stations broadcast the stories about atrocities to average citizens, people just trying to survive from paycheck to paycheck, people who had so little say in politics anymore.*

In fact, even if women had a bit more say than a hundred years ago, voting at the polls didn't seem to make much difference, not with the narrow selections between one rich man and another. Of course, this year, voters might be able to select a woman. But that woman seemed to be no more than Dick Cheney in drag to Judith. The words, "Whitewater" and "Vince Foster" still haunted her, even if it'd been more than a decade since she'd first heard them. Now, some man named Traveres, a crazy who'd murdered his mother, made death threats about Newt Romney, a Republican Presidential candidate. But Judith worried more about the 18-year-old Alabama girl, Natalie Holloway, abducted in Aruba a year and a half ago by three men, two of them brothers. She'd never remembered seeing so many abductions leading to rapes and murders within the past two years. Three of the women had been from the Kansas City area, too. The victims weren't necessarily from poor families or very rich, either. Many were middle class. In fact, one victim—Overland Park teen, Kelsey Smith, had been the daughter of a policeman.

Although most of the victims were teens, one of them, Summer Shipp, had been in her forties or maybe fifties, she couldn't remember for sure now. But the woman had a grown daughter, Brandy, who was now suing three companies that had hired her mother to do the door-to-door surveys she was performing when she was abducted and murdered. It seemed the world had gone crazy, especially in Kansas City. Of course, Kansas City had been a corrupt town, even long before her parents were born. During the 1920s and 1930s, it had been considered the most corrupt city in the nation, if not the world. In the 1920s, slot machines proliferated, even lined up in delis. And during Prohibition, in a bathtub at the LaSalle Hotel, men concocted mixtures they sold in the black market as "Gordon's gin." The Union Station massacre when mob members attacked feds who escorted gangster Frank Nitty, left passersby dead on the concrete.

Even at the turn of the twentieth century, corruption ran wild in Kansas City, known as a "Rip-Roarin' Town." Tom Pendergast, the proverbial Robin Hood, who'd sent a little girl a doll because her parents couldn't afford to buy her one for Christmas, had also absconded with funds from the public coffers, and had hired his concrete company to pave the city's sewers. And his temper was something, too: He'd thrown a stapler at people who'd angered him, including Harry Truman. Finally, Pendergast went to prison for tax evasion and spent most of his time there in an infirmary. The Kansas City gods punished him with ill health there. Judith wondered if his malady were similar to what ailed Paris Hilton during her stay after a DUI conviction. Perhaps the trauma of incarceration—or the shock of learning that all their power and fame hadn't sheltered them completely from the law—had created their illnesses.

Now, the newscasters talked about more murders and crashes on the highway, including one that killed a mother and badly injured her eleven-year-old daughter. Although Judith felt especially relieved that they'd avoided a wreck, she hated to see so many people suffering on the highways. It was bad enough that gas prices had skyrocketed, but the city's lack of good public transportation had forced too many people onto the roadways every day. And too many wrecks resulted, too many crashes resulted from some greedy CEOs and politicians' priorities. What did they care? She wondered. All the common people meant nothing to them, even though that's how they made their billions and collected their votes—from the masses of people who suffered because of these leaders' greed. It just made Judith ill to think about it, so she clicked off the television, not even waiting to hear the weather report.

She picked up a magazine and thumbed through it. A two-page photo spread stopped her. In the foreground, huge tree limb spread across the earth with a seat from a car beside it. In the background were houses, some without half their roofs, others in various states of disrepair. The headline read, "Katrina: The Untold Story." She closed the magazine and slammed it to the coffee table. Had nothing joyful happened the last few years? It seemed all she heard about were abductions and rapes, wrecks, wildfires, hurricanes, and flood—nothing but destruction—and that ubiquitous "War on Terror." What had happened to *fun* anyway? Where had it gone? After her brush with death that day, she felt like celebrating. But she didn't necessarily want to drink, so there was no celebrating with Mick. He worked closing shift tonight anyway.

She looked again at the stack of red, black, and blue—color-coded for each class—portfolios of student essays. There was no getting around it, she needed to grade them. But first, she'd read a few poems by Czeslaw Milosz. He'd certainly experienced more scenes of death and destruction that she had. Still, he'd created beauty amid all the horror. Somehow, too, he could incorporate that horror without transforming the poem into something ghastly or Gothic, like an Edgar Alan Poe piece.

She flipped through his *Selected Poems* and stopped at page 53, "The Poor Poet."

The first movement is singing.
A free voice, filling the mountains and valleys,
The first movement is joy,
But it is taken away.

And now that the years have transformed my
         blood
And thousands of planetary systems have been
         born and died in my flesh,
I sit, a sly and angry poet
With malevolently squinted eyes,
And weighing a pen in my hand,
I plot revenge.

I poise the pen and it puts forth twigs and leaves,
         it is covered with blossoms
And the scent of that tree is imprudent, for there,
         on the real earth,
Such trees do not grow, and like an insult
To suffer humanity is the scent of that tree.

Some take refuge in despair, which is sweet
Like strong tobacco, like a glass of vodka drunk
     in the hour of annihilation.
Others have the hope of fools, rosy as erotic
     dreams.

Still others find peace in the idolatry of country,
Which can last for a long time,
Although little longer than the nineteenth
century lasts.

But to me a cynical hope is given.
For since I opened my eyes I have seen only the
     glow of fires, massacres,
Only injustice, humiliation, and the laughable
     shame of braggarts.
To me is given the hope of revenge on others and
     on myself,
For I was he who knew
And took from it no profit for myself.

                    WARSAW, 1944

Judith read the words and sighed. Then she smiled, especially at the "malevolently squinted eyes."

Obviously, it was neither a "cheerful" poem, like the sort her mother liked, nor the epic sort of poem or nature poem that Mick preferred. Mick, at least, could give her more useful feedback on her poetry than her mother could. No, Milosz didn't write a cheerful poem here that celebrated life. Nevertheless, it was playful, and ironically, it gave her hope. In fact, it inspired her to write poetry again, even if she wouldn't likely win a Nobel Prize. After all, here was a man, born in a rustic environment, who'd risen to become a world-renowned poet, a Nobel prize-winning poet.

Milosz had grown up in a remote section of Lithuania, living in another century—a pre-technological world, a man who later witnessed the horror of the Polish version of the Holocaust, and he managed to weave his experiences into beautiful forms. *How—O how—could she do the same?* She wanted so much to weave her strange, surreal life into art—into something beautiful and meaningful, something that would cause readers to think, not a soap opera. Nevertheless, it seemed that every time she tried to capture her life's surrealism, it never came across.

Suddenly, she heard someone knocking on the back door. She couldn't figure out who would knock on that door—and not the front. She flew through the kitchen, peeked through the kitchen window, and saw Jenny, the robust woman from across the street. An excellent pianist and avid church-goer, Jenny had been friendly the first few years after Judith had moved into the neighborhood. She'd called Jenny to get together for coffee, and often brought over Danish pastries for the two of them to munch while they sipped their caffeinated drinks. But Judith hadn't seen Jenny much the past year or so, and she'd worried that she'd done something to offend her. In fact, for weeks now, when Judith drove somewhere and passed by Jenny in her yard, she hadn't waved the way she used to do. Then she'd heard Jenny was going through marital difficulties, so she attributed her odd behavior to the stress the woman must have been suffering. Jenny had been married to her husband Jake for more than twenty years. Judith had envied her for that long commitment.

"I figured you'd be in the kitchen," she said in her raspy voice. Judith often wondered how Jenny had such a wonderful singing voice when her speaking voice ranged between a raspy, garbled sound and a screech. "That's why I came here."

"Actually, I was in the living room, trying to psyche myself up to start grading."

"Oh, I'm sorry." Jenny screwed her face into an exaggerated frown with her bottom lip sticking out like the 1930s child star Shirley Temple did in her early movies when she often played a spoiled but amiable child, who often got her way by sticking out that lower lip. Today, Judith noticed how childish Jenny's features were, too. In fact, she wondered how she hadn't before perceived them. Perhaps, when Jenny was mainly depressed—without the mania she sometimes exhibited, she hadn't looked as much like a spoiled child.

"No. That's quite all right. I was just startled. Come in." Judith opened the door for the heavy woman who waddled into the kitchen. "Would you like coffee?"

"Actually, I wouldn't mind something stronger than that." Jenny laughed and pressed a hand on one of Judith's forearm. "Just kidding. It's just been a rough year. You knew Jake and I are getting divorced."

Judith nodded.

"It didn't bother me so much as long as JJ's been staying with me. But now, since he's turned twelve, Jake thinks it's better if he lives with him. It is probably better for JJ." Jenny crossed her arms. "But boy—I get so lonely." She sighed and then plopped into a chair by the kitchen table. She brushed off her lap as if there were crumbs on it. Judith thought it a bit odd. On the other hand, perhaps the woman just did it as a nervous habit.

"Hey, give me a call." Judith poured a cup of coffee and slid it in front of Jenny. "If I'm not busy teaching or grading, we can hang out for a while."

Jenny brightened, but something about her eyes made Judith uncomfortable.

Later, she learned why. In fact, it wasn't more than two weeks later when Judith came to regret her offer. At two a.m. on a Friday night, Jenny phoned from a hospital and asked for a ride home. Even if it was not more than fifteen minutes away, the demographics weren't the same as her neighborhood. Judith was afraid to drive there this late.

"It's my diabetes," Jenny explained as she sobbed. Her voice was raspier and more garbled than usual. "I ran out of insulin and passed out. Jake brought me here earlier this evening, but we had to wait for the test results. And he had to go home to his place way out in Kansas. So he could only stay till ten or so."

Once again, Judith wished Sheila and her family hadn't moved. Even if she'd likely be the one to drive to pick up Jenny, Sheila would've accompanied her. Jenny would've likely phoned Sheila first. Then the two of them would have gone together to collect Jenny, just as they'd driven all the way to the Lake of the Ozarks to collect Sheila's mother-in-law Marge. This was after Jack, her father-in-law's Alzheimer's disease escalated until he went out of control. That day, they'd found Marge sitting in a pool of urine on her bedroom floor.

She'd seemed stunned. In the meantime, her father-in-law had been driving all around the Lake of the Ozarks, not knowing where he was going. Plus, they weren't sure because Marge never admitted it, but Sheila and Judith wondered if Jack had beat on her, too.

Sheila's husband Randy couldn't handle the situation. She and Judith weren't sure if he was living in denial about his parents or if he just wanted to avoid hassles. Either way, it was Judith and Sheila who rescued the elderly people and brought them to Kansas City, where they moved in with Sheila and Randy. Obviously, it was too crowded in the bungalow, so they sold the parents' house in the Ozarks and all went together to buy a large house in Overland Park, which was why Sheila no longer lived next door. Judith also knew Jenny had often relied on Sheila during situations like this one, and since Sheila wasn't available now, she felt compelled to agree to pick up Jenny, out of pity. She woke Mick, who cursed Jenny, told him where she was going, and slipped into her Saturn. Of course, driving there was frightening. At first, she'd worried about

moving through dark streets, where an assailant could
spring from bushes onto her car. Instead, because it had
rained earlier and water pooled here and there, the
streetlights' glare off the asphalt on 63rd Street nearly
blinded her as she headed toward Research Hospital's
emergency room, where Jenny waited.

She wasn't sure whether to feel lucky or not that
few vehicles ventured out then. Even the thinnest
shadows caused her to tense up even more than when
she'd first left the house.   Those thoughts of what
happened to Natalie, Kelsey, and especially Summer,
rattled around in her brains. Then, she couldn't find the
emergency room. It appeared someone had moved it
since the last time she'd been by there years before,
almost ten years, in fact, when Krystal was three, after
her former husband had tried to murder her and nearly
succeeded. He'd missed her heart by an inch when he
thrust a buck knife into her chest. Thinking about her
last trip to Research made her chuckle at the irony. Here
she was nervous about driving, about being attacked by
a stranger there, when the person who almost took her

life had lived with her eight years. Life was indeed ironic. Too often it was as twisted as the meat in the hamburger patties Mick slid onto the grill each day.

Finally, she spotted the circle drive that led into the emergency entrance, and there, within a glass foyer, sat Jenny, hands in her lap, with a large, heavy paper bag with handles next to her. With wavy hair in disarray, baggy jeans and oversized shirt, she resembled a bag-lady, Judith thought. When she neared the entrance, Jenny stood, picked up the bag and headed out the door.

"Thank you *so* much." Jenny started rattling as soon as she hopped into the car. "I was so scared. I just started shaking, and then, everything went black. I mean, first splotches of black appeared, then they all grew to together." Jenny opened her purse and pulled out a cigarette.

"Who found you?"

"JJ was there, waiting for Jake to pick him up to go with him for the week. So when Jake arrived, they brought me here—hours ago. Jake stayed as long as he could. In fact, he thought the doctor would have me stay

the night. But I wanted him to release me." Her fingers
and arms shook as she puffed on her cigarette.

"So this happened from not taking your insulin?"

"Yeah. And well, I hadn't taken my lithium,
either."

"Lithium?"

"Yes, I'm bipolar."

"Why didn't you take it?" Judith tried to keep her
vision straight ahead. But the word *bipolar* rattled
around in her head. That meant Jenny was manic-
depressive. That meant she should never go off her
medication.

"I'm trying to lose weight." Jenny opened the
window and flicked her cigarette butt to the street. "I
can't get a man like this. I'm sixty pounds overweight."
She hesitated for a minute. "I want your figure."

Judith didn't know what to say, and the creepy
feelings that she'd occasionally felt when Jenny
suddenly flooded her with strange statements, perhaps
meant to be compliments, returned again. She didn't
know how to respond to such comments, and she'd say

nothing. In her uneasiness, she glanced at her watch. "Lord, it's after three a.m."

Jenny had begun humming. "You're a real life-saver. I owe you."

"It's okay," Judith sighed. "But next time, call during the day."

And the next time, she did. In fact, she stopped by Judith's house one morning when Judith was grading the day after classes had ended for Christmas break. This time, Jenny needed a ride to some space off Interstate-435 and Stadium Drive. Judith had little faith that she could even find the place.

"Why on earth do you need to go there?" She was sure Jenny could read her expression of disdain.

"That's where the city impounds cars. My Volvo's there."

"Did you wreck it? Park it in a towing zone?"

"No." Jenny stared at her feet. "Well. If I tell you, please don't get mad at me."

Judith crossed her arms. "Look—you stomp over

here asking me to drive to a place that scares me. I'm already angry. Plus, if you want me to take you there, you better explain why your car's there. *Pronto.*"

"I let Eddy use it." Jenny frowned and stuck out her lower lip. Eddy was the lover Jenny had taken into her house. Even though he supposedly made good money working on construction jobs, he seemed to drain her finances. Or Judith wondered if Jenny had been lying to Judith the past few weeks when she'd borrowed five dollars here, a ten-spot there. And one evening, she'd come over to ask Judith for aluminum foil to make a "pipe," she'd claimed. Judith wondered if Jenny and Eddy were smoking more than pot—perhaps they were into crack, which could explain the money drain and Jenny's sudden weight-loss. At least, she'd always repaid Judith. If she hadn't, Judith had vowed to herself she wouldn't loan Jenny money again.

"I wouldn't ask you, but Jake's on a business trip. It's so important that I get it out of there—"

"And how did it get impounded?"

"Eddy was high one night, so he didn't want to

drive it. You see, he does use his noggin sometimes. Anyway, he left the car in a parking lot, and the police towed it."

"Why isn't Eddy getting it?"

"He has to work. And the lot's only open during week days. He gave me the money to get it released."

Judith frowned. "And well he should."

"He gave me extra for gas, too. I'll pay you $15 for the ride."

"That isn't the point." Judith draped an arm around Jenny. "Look, I understand that you're lonely and you like this guy, but really, Jenny. I'm not sure he's very good for you. You have your own problems. You don't need to go cleaning up his messes."

"It's kind of my mess, too. I need my car."

"I'll drive you there on one condition: you never let him use your car again, okay?"

Jenny nodded, and her fingers quivered as she pulled a cigarette out and lit it.

"I'm not kidding. If I find out you let him use it—we're finished. I can't be your friend any longer."

Although the rescue ride to the hospital had been clean and quick, the ride to the police impoundment lot was the opposite. Once they exited the interstate, they wandered around Stadium Drive for an hour before they found the lot. Along they way, they ran over a bump that worried Judith. She hoped it hadn't damaged the Saturn—or caused the new gas cap to loosen. In fact, once they stopped, she checked it.

At least, the gate was unlocked, and Jenny could go retrieve her car.

"Will you come with me?"

"I need to pick up Krystal from school. The car will start, won't it?"

"I think so." She frowned. "I just don't want to talk to the policemen alone."

Judith glanced at her watch. "I'm running late. I'm sure they'll understand. Let them know you weren't the one who parked it there. Maybe you'll get off without a fine."

Judith sighed as she watched Jenny enter the building. She noted her wobble that had remained, even though Jenny had lost over twenty pounds. Still, she wore oversized men's shirts and baggy jeans, neither of which displayed her new figure. Judith hoped the woman would get home okay. If the car wouldn't start, she had a bevy of policemen to whom she could stick out her lower lip and beg for help. They'd probably be more useful than she could be, and certainly, they would be more flattered by Jenny's helplessness than she was. Nevertheless, Judith vowed to herself she'd phone her later to ensure Jenny had arrived home safely.

Besides, she wasn't quite sure how to get out of the area and back toward home. She'd have to wind her way away from Stadium Drive, a two-lane street—more like a highway really—that meandered through rows of thick maples and oaks that grew in dark clusters, creating miniature forests surrounded by pastures and streams, lovely rustic areas certainly, and areas that would make wonderful sites for frolicking with others on a picnic or hike, but nevertheless, not areas where a woman could risk spending any time alone, not even a minute, or she could end up like Summer, a woman who wasn't a teenager, a woman older than Judith was. Yes, somehow, she had to zoom through this area as fast as possible, hightail it west, where if something had damaged the Saturn when she flew over the bumps in the crazy, winding road, she could let someone look at it in an area where she felt relaxed, safe, an area less than a half-mile from State Line Road, an area several miles from where she was now.

Chapter Twelve
Adam's Plan

Finally Adam had pieced together the cuts of songs onto one tape, which he hoped he could transfer onto a CD, then save it in his computer. His mother had especially liked the lyrics to one of them, "Happy Dan's Fall-Out Shelter."

"It's so funny—in an ironic way." She laughed and told her friends about it.

He had to admit his mother's friend Jenny was quite an accomplished musician—she'd attended Julliard, after all. Judith encouraged him to learn a little about theory from her. But the woman was too wacky. One day, he tried visiting Jenny when she played on the organ and sang. Her voice wasn't bad, but it seemed frail, like a thirteen year old girl's. Of course, some rock groups liked that sound.

But her songs seemed to drag without varying the tempo much. And the way she sang her love lyrics in a breathy voice gave him the willies. Just the same, she was her mother's friend, and he felt a little sorry for her. So he remained kind.

"How do you like it?" Jenny asked after performing her newest love song. She smiled. "I wrote it for Eddy."

"Interesting." Adam nodded. "I'm curious about why you used so many diminished chords.

She tilted her head to the left and seemed to gaze out the window. She spoke in her usual raspy voice. "Well, you know, love is so sad, really. So painful. So the diminished chords bring out that feeling, don't you think?"

Adam shrugged. He didn't tell her the love song sounded more like a dirge. Even though he agreed that love could be difficult, he wrote them—the few love songs that he did write—in far more upbeat rhythms.

It wasn't that he didn't understand her battles with depression. His love life had fluctuated more than the stock market. Plus, he wore black and gray clothing long before the Goth look hit the scene. Moreover, he'd generally been quite open about his "dark side." In fact, he'd named his group, "The Morticians." But the group's songs didn't sound like dirges. That was the irony of it, they agreed. They merely liked ending their act by climbing into coffins.

His mother had helped him enroll in a music theory class at the local university's conservatory, and Adam had thrived in it. In fact, the professor had talked to his mother once on the phone. "Do you realize how talented your son is?" she'd said, at least, according to his mother. The professor had wanted him to audition for a scholarship. In fact, she'd offered to help him prepare for it, and a part of him wanted so much to try. Another part of him feared auditioning. If he were rejected, it'd dash his dreams. Then the professor finished her Ph.D. and moved to teach at another university several states away. Even though she'd still recommended Adam for a scholarship at the conservatory, Adam figured it'd be no use to go for it. It'd be so competitive, he was sure. So he hadn't filled out the reams of forms to apply. Besides, he wouldn't have time to work and complete a regular course load. Just doing the music theory class and working at the Haven took all his time. He couldn't imagine taking fifteen—or even twelve—hours of classes and working at least thirty hours a week. He didn't understand how other people managed that. Indeed, his mother had managed that. Of course, he hadn't seen that it'd done her much good. She didn't make that much money with a master's degree—and numerous hours beyond, almost enough for a doctorate. What good was it to work that hard and then not make even a decent living?

Now, she'd taken the LSAT and the law school had admitted her. Maybe this was her chance to achieve her dream—become a high-powered lawyer earning bundles of money. He had to admire her for that: such a tough hurdle. He wondered if she'd make it. His mother worked hard, but law school was a bitch. In fact, although he liked Socratic questioning, no way did he want to work that hard just to get a degree. Life was too short to waste it being so stressed out.

That's why he loved music. Perhaps it was work, too, but it wasn't like work because he became so wound up in it—even in developing schemes and patterns for music theory exercises—that the hours passed without him thinking about them. At that thought, he chuckled. The timing of the music had engulfed him so much that he'd become lost in time. Like Billy Pilgrim. But he hadn't suffered post-traumatic stress disorder from any war.

And unlike Billy Pilgrim, he didn't want to be stuck in some eyeglasses-salesman job. No, he didn't want to be stuck in any corporate position—no matter how high status it might be. In fact, although his mother's brothers were doctors and although he'd memorized the names of all the bones in the human skeleton and had begun memorizing the muscles, he didn't want to go into medicine, either.

Teaching would be a pain, too, unless—yes—unless he taught music. Anything concerning music gave him energy. Yes, that was his passion. It was just so tough here to make a living from it. Joe and his friends made hardly anything from gigs, even at the clubs. No, performing wouldn't get it in this city. He'd have to go national—cut a CD.

Chapter Thirteen
Mick Makes a Friend

Rod had been a God-send, Mick was sure. The kid worked hard, but he knew how to party, too. And Mick especially liked the way he showed him respect, something that Adam and Krystal rarely did. Within only six months, he'd come to view Rod as something similar to a son. So Rod and an Indian guy, a Kiowa named George, started coming by Mick's house after work. This was good, too, especially since Judith spent so much time at school or studying law books when she was home that she didn't pay much attention to him.

Rod had helped him out the previous summer, too, when Judith had decided a party would celebrate her admission to law school. The previous owners of their home had left behind an outdoor spa, a whirlpool actually, which no longer worked. But Mick and Rod decided, the Plexiglas spa would make a perfect tub for holding beer and soda cans packed on ice. But before they could use it, someone needed to scrub the thing. Rod volunteered and spent hours scouring the tub until it was cleaner than the kitchen counters. Mick was proud of the kid and paid him for it. Judith thanked him, too, but chided Mick for not helping him.

"You're treating that kid like a slave," she'd whispered after Rod went back to scrubbing. "He's your employee. You can't just use him as your personal servant."

"I'm paying him for it." Mick gulped a hit from the Michelob he clutched. "Out of my own pocket. He wants to help. He's a hard worker and can use the dough."

Both he and Rod cooked the burgers and chicken fillets on the grill, too. It was more like this party was his just as much as it was Judith's. People kept coming up to them to fill their plates, and everyone laughed and talked with him as much as they did with Judith, Adam, and Krystal.

Besides that, Mick was glad he had some of his buddies at the gig where Judith's idiot musician friend again performed. Mick didn't trust that guy Joe, but he was unsure why. At least, this year, with Rod and George there, Mick felt free to let loose and have a good time. So he drank and even danced until he became dizzy.

Then after the party had gone on for about an hour, Judith came flying out of the house and asked if he'd seen her checkbook. "I left it on the banister upstairs," she said, her voice shaky, and she scrutinized the guests. "I stuck $400 in it to deposit tomorrow. I just had it out. Now, I can't find it anywhere."

"I've been outside, Babe." Mick blinked. That was way too much money to lose. Even if it wasn't his, he knew he'd suffer for it if it didn't show up. "I ain't seen it. But I'll ask around." She looked a long time at Rod and George. Judging from her expression, she didn't suspect them but hoped they'd seen the checkbook.

None of them had seen it. "We've all been outside here—me, and Rod, and George," Mick said.

"Oh. Well, I have no money to pay the band tonight, either." She looked around again and went back inside. He asked Rod to bring him another beer.

Later, when the band was on break, Rod stepped inside the kitchen. He saw Joe talking with Judith, who was apologizing for not having the cash to pay him.

"It's okay," Joe had said. "I know you're good for it." He patted one of her arms.

Judith shook her head. "I don't get it. Everyone I asked here is my friend. No one would do that to me, not any of my guests. I just don't understand—" Mick saw Judith stare when Jenny and her boyfriend Eddy stepped into the kitchen from the dining room entrance. Jenny and Eddy made a strange couple. Jenny was still plump, and Eddy was small-built and skinny. In fact, he was scrawnier than Mick, or so, Mick thought.

Suddenly, he watched Judith smile stiffly, too. Suddenly, everything made sense. He hadn't trusted Eddy any more than he'd trusted Joe. And Judith's goofy girlfriend Jenny was pretty whack-o, too. Mick lumbered over to the couple and sat on a railing nearby.

"Where've you been hiding?" he asked.

"Oh, hi, Mick," Jenny gushed and nearly slobbered on his arm.

"Who's your friend?"

"You haven't met Eddy?"

He shook his head.

Eddy seemed to look him over, too, and Mick felt anger surge in his chest and spread down through his arms. This had to be where Judith's checkbook went. He could tell just by the way the guy darted his eyes and rubbed his nose. "Enjoying yourselves?" Mick forced a grin and stiffly lifted his hand to shake Eddy's. "I've seen you around. So you're our new neighbor?"

"Yeah." Eddy shrugged. "For a while, anyway."

"It's a good neighborhood." Mick withdrew his hand and crossed his arms. "Kind of like a family."

"Really?"

"We like to look out for each other, you know."

Mick squinted.

Eddy looked down at his feet. "That's cool."

"Hear you work construction. That's a good place to be these days. Good money, ain't it?"

Eddy shrugged. "Guess so."

"Yeah, it's kinda sad to see laborers get paid so well—I mean, not that they don't deserve it," Mick said then grinned. "But it just doesn't seem fair when teachers who have to go to school for so many years, like Judith, have to struggle so hard to make ends meet. They get paid a pittance compared to us."

"Hey. Life sucks." Eddy shrugged again.

Mick looked at him a long time, noted his deep-set eyes, stringy hair, and baggy, sagging jeans. He didn't like his smell, either. It was something heavy, like Jade East. He wondered why if the guy worked construction, he wasn't more muscular. The guy was a sleaze-bag, Mick was sure. He glared at him once more before he walked back outside and looked for Rod and George.

When he told Rod he figured he'd found the thief, Rod stared and grew silent for a while. Then his eyes glimmered as he spoke in a whisper. "What do you want me to do, Sir?" Rod rose to full attention. "George and I can take care of him, if that's what you want."

"Hey—what are you saying? You're a good Catholic boy."

Rod nodded. "Yes Sir. But I know when someone's been wronged, someone has to make things right. That's what being a soldier is about. That's what being a man is about." Then he stopped and smiled. "At least, that's what I've been taught."

"You're a good man, Son." Mick patted him on the back. "Good people."

Then he glanced from side to side, checked the back door, and spoke in a whisper. "When he steps outside, I'll point him out to you. If he's afraid to come back here, I'll show you where he lives, too. He's been sponging off one of the neighbor woman—a recent divorcee." Then Mick stopped talking a second. "And well, we'd like to get Judith's money back. But don't do more than rough him up a bit. No alienation, okay?"

With that, Mick slapped Rod's back again and

walked to the other side of the deck. He flipped over a few more burgers sizzling on the grill. Even if he hadn't gotten back to them as soon as he'd planned, the burgers had stayed thick and juicy.

He glanced back at Rod and George who kept looking at the back door then at him, as if they watched for his signal. Yes, it was good to have friends again, someone he could count on. The last time he'd had buddies like this was in the army. God, he hoped Rod wouldn't be transferred back to the Gulf. He needed him here, not just in the store, in his life. He needed someone on his side, someone with family values, yet someone who wasn't afraid to get tough to protect him and his family. Rod was the man—and George, too. He hoped they stayed at the Haven forever.

As soon as Eddy stepped outside, Mick nodded to Rod. Jenny had followed her date out into the back yard, so Mick stepped in front of her.

"You eaten yet?" He smiled broadly. "I've got low-fat grilled chicken—and of course, burgers. One of them has your name on it."

Jenny's eyes lit, and she followed Mick around to the grill.

Meanwhile, Rod and George closed in on Eddy and quietly nudged him around to the front driveway. Mick didn't see what happened, but he heard a car door slam and the roar of Rod's Camaro firing up. Then he heard him burn rubber as he left the drive.

Chapter Fourteen
Krystal Goes to Law School

The coolest thing about law school is that many cute guys go there. Most of them seem to like me, too, and I think some of them think I'm old enough to date. So when I wait for Momma after she picks me up from school, I always read novels. That way, no one can tell what grade you're in. At first, I didn't wear my plaid skirt on those days. Instead, I wore the uniform slacks that the school allows. But later, I saw some of the women in law school wearing Catholic school tartan skirts, so once in a while, I wear mine. I still have most of them fooled, that is, unless they know Momma. In fact, a couple of guys have let me know they believed I was a law student.

They asked me about torts and contracts classes. Yesterday, one of them—a cute guy with dark brown eyes and hair—was sure I was in one of his classes. I shook my head but didn't let him know that I didn't attend this school. And then, one of the deans is always asking me to eat from the free fruit bowls and cheese trays they set up for law school parties. So I think he believes I'm a law school student, too, especially later, after I appeared in one of the law school's plays called the *$1.98 Law Review*. The students hold it every spring. It was my début as an actress.

You see, some good has come from Mick's rotten actions. Ever since Mick pulled his last trick, Momma's been taking me everywhere with her, and I'm glad. No way do I want to be alone with Mick again—not ever. In fact, I wish Momma made enough money so she could divorce him. I think that's why she's trying law school, so she can support Adam and me without any man helping her. Even though my dad sends her money, Momma says it isn't nearly enough, especially because I attend a Catholic school. But Momma's determined that

I stay in one, so there's no way she'll cut corners about that. Now that I'm fourteen and in high school, I understand why she won't let me attend public schools. In Kansas City, they're the pits. In fact, the Kansas City School District lost its accreditation. Momma said busing contributed its downfall. Of course, other things caused it, too. But Momma stressed that it wasn't the teachers. She'd seen the syllabi for Adam's classes the year he went to Southwest. "They're good teachers," she'd claimed, "locked in a horrible situation."

I hope Momma finds another guy here, too, so she can leave Mick before she graduates. Otherwise, I'll have to wait four more years, not just three. You see, even though the law school admitted Momma as a full-time student, she decided that wouldn't work. Momma still teaches a class at the community college and edits a magazine, even though the law school dean wanted her to quit everything and focus only on law school classes. Momma told her she couldn't afford to do that, not with two kids living at home. So the dean let her into the "flex" program, which was kinda "part-time."

But Momma says it isn't truly part-time because she has to take at least three classes, as much as she'd take in regular graduate school. And she says the classes are harder than any she's ever taken, especially because she didn't take any "pre-law" classes as an undergraduate. But she also said that working as a newspaper reporter and writer have helped her more than anything, except perhaps analyzing literature and maybe doing crossword puzzles. Being a reporter taught her to write for an audience, she explained, "even if the audience sometimes comprised idiots."

Anyway, one of the guys that she studies with seems to like her, I mean, as more than just a friend. He plays the guitar, too, the bass actually, and was in a band in his home town just outside St. Louis. His name's Mitchell, but everyone calls him by his last name, Tanner. Even I call him Tanner. He just doesn't seem like a Mitchell. Well, Tanner and his group, called Long Shot, cut a CD. They sound a bit like the group Cure, but not quite as good. Still, I like listening to their music with Momma while we do dishes. And Momma brings me along with Tanner when they take a break for dinner at Winstead's. I like that, especially because Momma doesn't seem to mind what I eat then. I can have all the French fries I want, with lots of ketchup.

"Hey, Pretty Lady," he said to Momma the last time we met him there. He winked at me and smiled broadly, so maybe he was calling both of us pretty. I'm not sure, but he watches Momma a lot and pays more attention to her than me when we eat together or go to The Flea Market Restaurant and play Foos Ball. See, some of the guys here don't. In fact, they talk to me more than Momma. But not Tanner.

He'll wave his arms and smile too much and open his eyes wide when he talks with her, and lean his head in close to hers, as if they were conspirators in an agency. When they first met with a group of law students in Flannigan's in Brookside, Tanner blabbered away, telling her about his days growing up in a small town, flying airplanes, and getting into jams that almost killed him. I was surprised Momma didn't mention a couple of her death-defying feats, such as lately, when the Saturn abducted us. Oh no—she just smiled and giggled, and glowed. In fact, she glowed so much it seemed a halo surrounded her. It wasn't like the halos on Christmas cards above Baby Jesus and Mary. Instead, it glimmered all around her head with spikes of energy fluttering in every direction, like sunrays. Actually, it was more like an aura.

One Sunday afternoon in November, the week after Thanksgiving, Tanner, Momma, and I met in the law library. I was reading *Pride and Prejudice* for about the hundredth time, and Momma and Tanner studied property law outlines, from which they'd create questions. Mainly, they went over the various common laws in property, such as the law of **adverse** possession. Now, that law is kinda cool. See, if a person owns some land but doesn't live on it and another person comes along and basically squats on it—you know, either takes over an abandoned house or builds one. Then, if the person waits there twenty years—ten in some states, the person can record a deed and owns the land. But if the original owner comes on the land every so often, and politely reminds the squatter just who owns the land and reminds the squatter he, the owner—not the squatter—is giving him permission to use it, then the squatter can't own the land. Momma said she saw this happen in the mountains in Breckenridge, Colorado. People in their twenties would come across abandoned cabins when they were hiking, and if they were hanging around in the area, before you know it, they'd start living in those cabins.

When the owner finally came by, probably he was a mustached, white-haired guy riding a roan or maybe an Appaloosa, he'd say, "Welcome." And he'd likely turn on his saddle and point to some logs. "Go ahead and use them, too. But be sure the fire's completely out before you leave the cabin."

Well, the kids would whoop and holler about what a nice guy the land-owner was for letting them live rent-free on his land. But the truth was, he was protecting his property rights in two ways:

- He'd remind them that he owned the land, and

- He let them squat; then, so no **adverse** possession occurred.

It just seems all the property moguls are clever that way. They can go around seeming like nice guys, when really, they're just holding onto their real estate. Momma studied this, and it seemed she pushed Tanner to study a bit more than he wanted. He was a smart guy, but he didn't very care much about what sort of grades he made in law school, just so he passed. In fact, the only reason he probably spent so much time studying that first semester was because he wasn't sure he would pass. Still, he joked about grades a lot.

"C + C + C equals J.D.," he'd repeat, especially right before an exam, even when they were in heated study. Or he'd say, "The A students become teachers, the B students become judges, and the C students, the C students make the most money." Considering Momma's grades and finances, I kinda wondered if he wasn't right—and not just about the law school world. Sometimes, it seemed the entire world was like that, too. Still, Momma wouldn't share Tanner's attitude about grades. When he would joke about them, Momma would shake her head. "For you, maybe. But I don't plan to be a street lawyer—not that there's anything wrong with that. I just don't want to be a litigator. Life's enough of a battle without bringing on more. I need to work in the courts—for a judge or something like that."

But even Tanner especially liked these sorts of property laws, laws that were kinda tricky. Even though he'd laugh at the situations in criminal or tort law, it seemed he especially liked laws concerning money or real estate. And it seemed studying about property fired up his imagination. Like today, right in the middle of one of his and Momma's rote memorization sessions, he did goofy things.

He smiled broadly, till he looked like a frog who'd just snapped a fly. "Yep, on the very day I finish with this school, I'm going to buy me an Armani suit and a pair of Doc Martens." He leaned back, crossed his legs, and stretched them so his feet rested on the end of the library table. "And then after I'm set up in business, I'm going to hire me a secretary who'll make me coffee."

"Hffmphf!" Momma scoffed. "I hope he's a male." She looked at her property-class outline a second, frowned, then back at Tanner and squinted. "Besides, don't forget: First, you have to pass all your finals, then you have to pass your classes. And finally, you must pass the Bar."

Tanner smiled like a frog again, and then he leaned his head back as if he were snoozing. "No problem." He inhaled. "It'll be a cinch."

"Pride goeth before a fall," Momma said and returned to reading her book.

So they'd banter like that when they got together, and I always felt happy around them. I didn't feel that way much anymore when Momma and Mick were together. The first year they were married, I did. But it seems the longer they stayed together, the less often they had fun. And of course, that meant when I was with them, it wasn't as much fun for me, either. But hearing Momma and Tanner toss words back and forth made me laugh. I tried not to giggle, in case other students were around who might think I was just a high school kid.

Chapter Fifteen
Judith's Review

During the next fall, Judith worked on a law review about using stories—or narratives—in feminist jurisprudence. Researching cases and analysis was tough, but she found it went more smoothly once she finished her introduction, a narrative. She wrote a narrative about a friend she'd known in graduate school and her experiences in London. She'd been amazed at how rapidly she'd written the story—and it was a long one, too. It'd run nineteen pages in manuscript form. But it seemed as if the words flowed out more rapidly than they had for any story she'd written in graduate school, including her 330-page novel. Then, she worked on each sentence, chiseled each phrase, worried about each line of dialogue. Not so with the narrative. It went like this:

Caroline's Story

"If you look at life one way, there is always cause for alarm."

—Elizabeth Bowen, *The Death of the Heart* (1939)

"What is usually done may be evidence of what ought to be done, but what ought to be done is fixed by a standard of reasonable prudence whether it usually is complied with or not."

—Oliver Wendall Holmes, Jr. (*Texas and Pac. Ry v. Behymer* 1)

His coat flapping, a large, black-haired man with a square jaw charged down the escalator toward Caroline. The large overcoat made him look like a goose, but his hooded eyes weren't comical. She shivered then leaned further right. Vauxhall Station's escalators were narrow, and passersby brushed against each other. *Thud, thud, thud*—the bodies hit again and again as she rose to the second level. Although she shrank from the large man's shoulder, he shoved her anyway. His thick shoulder felt as hard as a cinderblock, and he smelled of sour rum—or perhaps an acrid aftershave.

"Sorry!" he snapped.

Sorry, always sorry. British men never said, "Excuse me." Sorry, it was, always—as if the situation couldn't be avoided and they were giving condolences. As if they felt no need to excuse themselves. And they spit out those words like stones, icy as hail. They said them automatically, without feeling, without thought.

Once more, she glanced around for Professor Darcy. Although she'd left Harrington Gardens alone, she'd spotted him in the Tube. Then she'd sunk lower in her seat so he didn't see her, but she worried he might catch her now in the station. And she didn't want to be with him alone again. She twisted her long, dark hair into a roll and stuffed it under her blazer collar, pulled out a mob-shaped knit cap, tugged it over her ears, and stepped outside. She shivered. The wet, heavy fog blurred the bright blues, yellows, and reds on the Tudor buildings lining the streets. London had surprised her. She'd anticipated the city would be gray, dismal with buildings covered in soot, and she'd expected this sort of weather. Instead, the buildings were colorful cottages— making the huge city appear to be a conglomeration of English villages, and this had been the first day the fog had set in since they'd arrived two weeks before. Perhaps the lively colors and warm, sunny days had thrown her out-of-joint—caused her to lower her guard. She should've known better.

On campus, she'd rather liked him. Head of the department where she was finishing her M.A. and teaching freshmen and sophomore classes, he'd always smiled when he saw her, always spurted out a cheerful hello. And his eyes lit each time she stepped into the department office. At the minimum, he appeared to be acutely aware of her presence: His sideward glances when he talked with someone else, the nervous twitter of a hand, implied as much. *This is good*, she'd thought. He was, after all, her boss. And often, she considered what colleagues had said: He's been known to keep teachers he likes after they graduate. Many of them receive full-time positions. *Best to stay on his good side.* She intended to teach at the university once she finished her degree, so she vowed she'd allow Professor Darcy no reason to dislike her.

And then, suddenly, the London study-tour popped up. She'd receive three hours of graduate credit for the English theater class, and finally, she'd explore the divine London she'd ached to visit since childhood. She'd signed up before she knew Professor Darcy would lead the tour. Even then, she hadn't minded. Many times after department meetings, she'd chatted with him and his wife at a neighborhood bar. They talked about more than teaching, too.

The Darcys owned a large, Quality Hill Victorian that they struggled to sell but were asking too high a price. She didn't tell them that, of course, but offered hints that had helped her sell her Leawood estate.

Mainly, the gatherings were the typical student-faculty *tête-à-têtes*. Nonetheless, the Darcys were an interesting couple, chatting about James Joyce, Robert Browning, and Jane Austen, and she especially liked discussing "Araby" and "My Last Duchess" with them. So she was happy to learn they'd be leading the trip. Then, Mrs. Darcy cancelled. And from the time they took off, Professor Darcy hovered around her.

At the Atlanta airport, he'd slapped his passport into her right hand, squeezed the brim of his golf cap, and grinned. "Remember—repetition." He winked. "Tell them we'll take first class. Repeat it. Get it into their subconscious. After all, the airline messed up our reservations."

He shrugged and scurried down the aisle. She looked at the passport. He was but eight years older than she was, but something made her feel as if he was part of another generation. She looked up from the book and glanced around the sepia airport. Most students had arrived. Linda and Katie, two women she knew from a contemporary drama class joined the line now forming behind her. Then, the professor reappeared as they neared the counter. He grinned again, and his eyes glistened as he leaned over it. "We booked reservations for eleven students and two teachers to London. Here's the confirmation."

Two ticket women rustled papers and spoke simultaneously. The reservations had been lost. He grinned once more. "Surely, you can fit us into first class," he commanded. "We'll take first class."

The women looked up and glared at him, glanced at Caroline, then looked back at Professor Darcy. He smiled. "First class will be fine." They picked up phone receivers, the professor continued yakking, and more papers flurried. Eventually, they seated the other professor and all the students—except Caroline—in business. They booked her with Professor Darcy in first class.

When they took their seats, Professor Darcy patted her on the back. "We did it!" He grabbed her left hand and squeezed it. "Stick with me, Carrie, and you'll go far." He laughed. She smiled at the ambiguity. His manipulation of the airline personnel had also impressed her. A part of her wished she had that power to control people.

After takeoff, Professor Darcy squeezed her knee. "Let's go back to the bar." He smiled, his black eyes glistening when he looked at her. They became pools of oil that reflected her stare. "You like Bailey's?" he asked.

"I don't know," she replied, embarrassed at her lack of sophistication. She hadn't known that first class passengers on overseas flights could amble back to a bar, where they could order whatever they wanted. "What is it?"

He chuckled. "A cream liqueur." His eyes glistened brighter. "Rich, smooth."

"Sounds good." She forced a smile and followed the professor to the bar.

"Two Bailey's, on the rocks." When he ordered, he wrapped an arm around her and pulled her to his side. She wondered if he saw her as his date. She now noticed that his voice emulated Gomer Pile's. Although

Professor Darcy's contained more of a Texas than a backwoods' drawl, the low, hollow sound, the empty, echoing tone, was the same. And the sound of that television character's voice unnerved her. So did Professor Darcy's.

His fingers weren't calloused, but they felt rough against hers when he handed her the icy concoction that looked like coffee-tinged milk.

"Thanks." She felt awkward but still looked up, smiled, and sipped her drink. It was rich and sweet. She reminded herself that no one had done anything out-of-line, anything off-color. Perhaps Professor Darcy's imperative personality merely had thrust her into a role she hadn't anticipated. If so, then, she'd play it—but only to a point. Adultery certainly wasn't on her agenda. And she had to remain friendly. Her future depended upon this man.

He sipped on a straw then used it to gig an ice cube. He crunched it, then laughed. "Whew! Bailey's. It's been awhile!"

"How often do you come to London?"

He smiled, squinted, and stared at her for several seconds. Then he gazed into the distance, rubbed his nose with a knuckle, and sighed. "It's been a long time—a very long time."

The professor ordered another round, and now, other first class passengers approached the bar. Some students slipped in from business class, too, and Professor Darcy grabbed his drink and lumbered to their table, where he spoke a few lines she couldn't decipher, then he laughed heartily, throwing back his head.

A man slid in next to her. "Hi there, honey. You from Atlanta, too?" Pot-bellied, with a gray mustache, he smelled like kerosene and wheezed when he spoke in his Mississippi drawl. He looped a thumb in his belt then rattled on about his tour plans.

She listened, sometimes smiled but shied away from his touch. Suddenly, the professor was at her elbow again, sliding an arm around her and clutching her more tightly this time, squeezed her against his body. "Let's go back to our seats and catch the movie," he said. She looked at him but said nothing. By then, she'd begun to feel a bit dizzy. *Top Gun* played on the airplane's screen. With the alcohol buzzing through her brain cells, she couldn't concentrate on the film. Instead, she scribbled happy traveler's clichés on postcards.

"Who's he?" the professor asked when he watched her scribble a man's name across one of the cards.

"A friend."

"Oh." He looked away and didn't talk for awhile. Then he went to the bar and returned with two more drinks. She sipped the next one very slowly, and indeed, the cream settled her stomach. Nevertheless, she wasn't used to drinking, let alone so much, and she felt her lips go numb.

More Irish Crèmes blurred the night. Movie images of airplane fights flashed before her, making her slightly nervous, and the professor chattered on, until finally, he slept. She tried very hard to sleep but couldn't.

The next day was more of a blur than the flight had been. Caroline had dozed just forty-five minutes during the six hours in the air, so her patience had already become frail when she waited in the line of students. They seemed to hike forever, their luggage in tow, through Heathrow and customs, onto the bus, and finally to their London home, the row house in Kensington Burrough. It was a beautiful stone building with a white, ornately carved, Victorian doorjamb, but it smelled musty, as if the dampness permeating its walls had remained there for a millennium. She roomed with Linda and Katie, and the threesome took all afternoon to unpack.

"First thing, I'm hitting the white sales," Linda said and drew a gown up to her chin while she stared in a mirror. A beautiful woman of forty or so, with black hair and huge brown eyes, she spent most of her paycheck on designer dresses that she'd find in bargain basements. "I never buy off the rack," Linda had once told a group of students. But Caroline knew her shopping buddy, who confided how Linda shopped. Moreover, Linda's bragging had little effect upon Caroline, who usually wore jeans or long denim skirts.

More casually dressed, shorter, and less attractive, frizzy-haired Katie wasn't as infatuated with clothes, which she hurriedly stuffed into a bureau. "And we're hitting the pubs every night," she chimed it. "If I can afford it, I'm taking in a concert, too."

Caroline said little. She hoped the two hadn't expected her to go traipsing with them everywhere. She'd planned to see the Tate, the Victoria and Albert Museum, the Victorian cottages and Gothic churches, the palaces, especially Kensington, and maybe hike to Piccadilly Circus. She could shop and drink at home.

Drowsy then, she'd rested her head on a pillow and had just dozed off when Professor Darcy and two male students, Jamey and Grant, knocked on the door.

"Let's go, girls--we're in London!" the professor said then tugged the pillow under Caroline's head. "What pub shall we frequent tonight?"

"I saw one in the brochure," Katie said."The Firkin."

The professor laughed. "Which one" There's the Falcon Firkin, the Flounder Firkin, the Fox Firkin, Frog

Firkin, Pheasant Firkin, Phoenix Firkin. I suppose somewhere, there's a Firkin Firkin."

"Can't we sleep first?" Caroline frowned and closed her eyes again."

But by that time, she couldn't sleep, not even after the men had cleared out. Linda hunted around for a table she could use as an ironing board, her roommates yakked on and on, and Caroline's stomach now ached. So when the men knocked on Door 138 again, she shooed the others out, and said, no, she'd stay in—she wanted to sleep. The truth was, she hadn't wanted to spend much money partying—she had souvenirs to buy, and she wanted money for touring and emergencies. Partying seemed such a waste. She'd started to relax for a few minutes. Then a soft knock sounded on the door.

"Carrie?" It was Professor Darcy. He stepped inside, stared at her, crossed his arms and frowned. "You're not going?"

She looked at the floor. "No. I'm tired, and well, I need to save my money for gifts." She looked at him and smiled. "I'm not much of a party person anyway." She turned away and leaned against the mantel, ornately carved in a Victorian leaf design.

"But you can't be anti-social. That could put a damper on the trip." Smelling of English Leather, he edged closer to her till his breath hit her cheek.

She smiled again. "Doubt I'll be missed. I don't add that much excitement to parties anyway. I'll go another night. I need to take it easy at first. Hey, I'm still a student and don't have that much—"

"You're a graduate assistant, right?" She looked at him. He grinned. "So I can have you as my assistant. Would $75 cover your gifts?"

"Well, uh, I'm not sure." She looked at the floor again. It was dark wood. His offer had startled her.

"Let's make it $100. Then you can charge that much in gifts and use your cash to socialize. You won't get the bill until a while after we return. The day after we're back, I'll submit a request for a stipend, and you can pay your Visa with it."

"Sounds good." She smiled. "I mean, if you're

sure it will be okay. I wouldn't want you to get into trouble."

He smiled, leaned his face toward her and looked into her eyes, his eyes glinting red now, and then he looked at her lips. Carrie said nothing but stepped back from him.

Suddenly, he stopped moving, glanced downwards, and sighed. He looked back in her eyes, smiled, and drew his fingers over one of her forearms. "So let's go to the pub."

The following weeks, he confused her even more. Especially in graduate school, she'd been close to many of her professors, including the men. They were friendly; she was friendly. Sometimes, they flirted; sometimes she did. But no one took any of this seriously. Certainly, she'd never slept with any of them. And none of them made her feel compelled to do so. She'd also made a point of earning any A's before she partied with a new professor. She wanted to be graded on her work—not on her personality. But before the Britain trip had ended, it seemed Professor Darcy had graded her exclusively on the latter.

"You're too focused—like my wife," he'd complained one evening when they strolled with the group to a theater, where they watched and later analyzed Ibsen's "Ghosts," Vanessa Redgrave playing the lead. "I might as well be with my wife."

She didn't argue but avoided him during intermission, and the following day, she toured with her roommates. That, too, had been a disaster. The trio had taken the Tube to a shopping district, and Caroline had been mulling over how to politely remove herself from the awkward situation with the professor. She didn't want to offend him. She wanted to remain friends with him—in fact, she wanted to relax around him—feel the freedom she felt around other colleagues. But that seemed to grow more and more impossible. As she pondered the situation and stared at the gray walls outside the underground's windows, the Tube came to their station.

"Let's go!" Linda yelled and headed toward the door. Startled, Caroline hopped up but forgot her journal. Linda spotted it and grabbed it, but then she stopped to scold Caroline severely. Because she spent so long in the aisle scolding, the Tube door closed just after Caroline stepped out. Linda couldn't leave and had to ride the Tube to the next station. Katie laughed and Caroline wanted to, but she didn't dare. After all, Linda had rescued her journal, so Caroline felt too guilty to chuckle. In fact, when Linda arrived on the returning Tube, she was so steamed that Caroline apologized profusely. She offered Linda two pounds for her trouble. Linda refused, and Caroline left the group. Touring the city alone would be safest for her, she was sure. More than Jack the Ripper, she feared alienating the others. She was too preoccupied to truly connect with them. Occasionally, the entire group would take a tour bus to Oxford or Bath, but most afternoons, after the class let out, Caroline strolled alone, ate salads and dark, Military chocolate bars at a gallery or sucked on a bittersweet Cadbury bar and metallic-tasting tea while she strolled the streets. Some evenings, though, she socialized a little with the group at the pubs. She especially liked one of the Firkins that served half-heads of cauliflower smothered in cheese. For seventy pence, she had her whole dinner.

Mornings, they sat in classes. But after the first class with Professor Darcy, Caroline had opted to solely listen—not discuss her thoughts.

"I don't know why graduate students are afraid to talk," he'd grumbled the first day. He twisted chalk in between his fingers then stared at Caroline. "Or they cough up clever quips, but they don't follow them with reasoned arguments."

"Perhaps they're insecure," she'd replied.

"So why don't they follow through?" His eyes glimmered into hot coals.

"Perhaps they're afraid of offending. You hold their futures in your hands. It's an awkward situation."

A couple of days passed, and after attending plays each evening, the group wanted a break—another pub outing. This time, Caroline stayed in to study. A little after eleven, the motley crew sang loudly in the hallway and clambered into her room. Katie and Linda plopped onto their beds, and Professor Darcy, Jamey, and Grant dropped into chairs. After finishing the round, "Ninety-nine Beers," Professor Darcy spoke. "Ibsen is the best nineteenth century playwright, don't you agree, Carrie?"

She looked up from her book. "Actually, I prefer Shaw."

"Over Ibsen? Why?" His voice was deep, more harsh than hollow now. He frowned and stroked his chin. A vein in his forehead throbbed.

She didn't care anymore if he disagreed. "Shaw sees the humor—man's foibles."

"Tragedy's the higher art."

"So Ari says." She smiled. "But comedy projects a more rational perspective, a more eternal perspective. It views humankind from a distance. *Misalliance* parallels the themes in *Ghosts*, but Shaw makes us take them less seriously."

"A typical woman's response—let us not take

things seriously," he snapped. His words became bullets. The vein on his forehead turned purple. He swooped an arm toward Jamey. "Let's not think too hard. Either that, or they take everything too seriously. They wallow in emotion, right, Jamey?"

Jamey shrugged, and Caroline left the room. Her stomach had started to ache, and it didn't settle for the rest of the trip.

His words ebbed and flowed from day-to-day like that, and now, her memory bloated with images—the professor striding beside her, a newspaper shielding his head from drizzle after the group had expected the Tube to run after midnight on New Year's Eve, and so everyone was doomed to hike seven miles in rain across London; earlier, his lingering gaze at her legs when she slipped into her "London ensemble": tall, black boots with a black sweater dress that hit above her knees; his thigh intermittently sliding against hers when they watched *Les Liaisons Dangereuses*, and last night, his curt words at the Chinese restaurant. The group had been talking about British women, and somehow the conversation slid into attractions, specifically whether romantic attractions were physical or spiritual.

"People can have spiritual relationships," she'd averred. "The spiritual's more meaningful than the physical."

"No," the professor had retorted. His cheeks grew red. "The physical's just as important." He'd slammed his teacup onto the table. Jamey and Grant stared at him. "You need both for a relationship to be complete."

Later, she almost gasped when he picked up the soup bowl and drank from its rim. She'd heard the Chinese drink egg-drop soup from small soup bowls, tiny ones, like rice cups. But the professor drank from a huge bowl—the size of a chowder bowl. Perhaps she was mistaken, but then it seemed the professor was less urbane than the Beverly Hillbillies. The ache in her gut grew into a ball of fire.

And this morning was the final insult. She'd awakened late, after the other students had left to traipse around the city. She didn't mind. In fact, she enjoyed having the ancient building to herself. But when she ambled into the kitchen, there stood the professor. He held a coffee cup, leaned against a table, and looked at her face. Then his gaze went to her breasts, where it lingered, on down to her hips and thighs and then up to her face again. A girlfriend of hers had once called such a look an "elevator stare." He'd grinned. "Good morning," he'd said. "You look enticing today." She'd forced a smile and had left. Later, she worried if her clothes had been seductive—but no. Her baggy sweater fell to her thighs, and her jeans were loose, too.

Now the fog grew into drizzle as she jaunted over Vauxhall Bridge toward the Tate. A yellow haze formed on the western horizon. It looked almost like the lip of a foaming wave rolling into shore. Yes, this was the London she'd seen in photographs, movies, and TV. She stopped at the railing and stared into the river. It looked deep and murky. The haze rose from it and enveloped her. It seemed to penetrate her. She felt trapped. She decided then she'd avoid the professor for the rest of the trip and the voyage home. How she'd make it through the nineteenth century lit class with him she was unsure, but somehow, she'd keep a low profile then, too. She'd wanted a friendship—a professional relationship—nothing more. Moreover, something was out-of-joint here. Something was wrong with this picture. And she couldn't figure out how to re-adjust it.

Not until after she'd returned to the states did she begin to see her life become a waterlogged plank that cracked and split into shambles. It began two days after the spring semester had started. Professor Darcy called her into her office.

Her hands trembled when she opened the door. "You sent a note?"

He looked up and didn't smile. He closed a manila folder and slammed it onto his desk, then he stood. "Yes. We need to talk." He strolled to the door that she'd closed, cracked it open, and swooped an arm over a chair. "Sit down."

He returned to his desk, plopped into his chair and clasped its arms. His knuckles grew white. "I can't handle having you in class." He moved his hands to the desk and began untwisting a paperclip, then wriggling it into a crinkled shape.

She'd stared at him then glanced at her knees. They, too, now shook. She looked back at him.

"I thought it'd be okay—but after the other night, no. I can't handle it." He stared at her a long time, as if he wanted some response that she could not discern, then he watched his fingers playing with the paperclip.

The other night? Apparently, he was alluding to the class. She'd said nothing in that class—done nothing but giggle at his *falsetto* rendition of Jane Austen's persona in the introduction of *Pride and Prejudice.* He was, indeed, funny. She couldn't help but chuckle.

"I know too much about you," he went on. "I don't think I can be a fair judge of—"

Knew too much about her? Since when did that bother a teacher? *But the reverse—ah, yes, the old male projection game. It was what she knew about him.* This bothered him. She frowned. "You want me to drop the class?"

He looked at the file on his desk, ran a forefinger around its edge. "It'd be better for everyone involved." He glanced at the door then at her. "You're an excellent student—incredibly perceptive. But we must walk the road of reason here." He sighed then grinned. "Hey, the fellow from New Zealand's teaching a class on Joyce. It isn't too late to sign up."

"James Joyce?"

"He did his dissertation on him. He's quite good." He grinned again now, more broadly. "And I've no problem with your teaching. Jan's given you an excellent evaluation, a high recommendation—and she's tough to please. Your student evaluations were very high, too."

"What about the theater class?"

"I just need to grade your paper. I'm okay with it."

Just like you said you'd be okay with the nineteenth century lit class, she thought but said nothing. After her doubts about him escalated throughout the London trip, she'd asked him about the class during intermission from *The Winter's Tale*. Then, he'd sipped Drambuie from a shot glass. "I have no problem with it." He'd shrugged, grinned, and tossed his head as if she were being silly.

Now, after this scene today, her fears ran deeper. No other universities were located near her. Where would she teach when she graduated?

After she left his office, she wound around the department building to a stone bench hidden amid spindly, leafless elms. She fell to the bench, her books tumbling onto the frozen ground, and she stared at the Nelson Gallery for a long time. The pain in her stomach returned.

When Caroline recounted her story to me, an oxygen tube linked her to a wall at Research Medical Center. No, the events that transpired in London did not lead her there—at least, not directly. And yet, she claims that is when her downward spiral started.

"I'd like to go back to England," she said then looked out the window. A film of liquid coated her eyes as she focused upon some distant structure. She looked back at me. "Things have plummeted since then: I discovered Jim beating my kid. A pervert exposed himself to me at 7-11, and now, Jim did this. It seems if a person retraces her steps to a turning point, she can reverse the cycle, like the way you can stop a microwave and spin a platter the other direction. So I need to return there so I can re-spin my life."

I smiled. Her homey analogies amused me, even if they sometimes failed to connect. Somewhat like now, when she had almost connected with death. A yellow tube linked her to a wall from which oxygen coursed through her ribcage and into her left lung. Her six-foot-four, 220-pound husband Jim had tried to stab her to death. His aim had been off—he'd punctured a lung and missed her heart by an inch. And today, her gaunt cheeks and glossy eyes made her look punctured, flat as an inner tube that couldn't stay afloat, even on tranquil waters.

She'd struggled three days, mulling over whether or not to press charges against Jim. He'd stabbed her, she said, because he didn't want a divorce. Although she was concerned about letting the madman off to perhaps repeat such a scene, other concerns refrained her from suing.

"Besides, just what is my debt to society?" she asked and again, twisted a strand of long, dark hair around a finger. "Don't I owe more to Elizabeth? How would having a father in prison impact her? Plus, the courts would lock him up for only a couple of years. He could return and kill me. I need the child support, too. Will society give me that—and lifelong protection?" She also worried about her career.

"What about Darcy?" I asked. "*Quid quo pro* sexual harassment? I'll check out some recent cases— *Meritor, Alexander.* They may be analogous. Perhaps innuendoes will be enough."

She sighed then smiled wryly. "Hopeless, isn't it? His word against mine. Who'd dare be a witness? I'm shocked that he kicked me out of class, especially after he kept sending me notes when we returned. But more than that, I'm worried that he'll quash my chances at a permanent job. Now, I really need it. What gives men the power to call all the shots—even these puny demigods who don't run a nation or a large corporation—just a small department in a small university, a purportedly equal opportunity employer? Why do they get by with this? What gives them the right? Can't the law—some law—stop them? And nothing actually happened in London. He came on to me. I didn't aggressively discourage him. But I was afraid to. I didn't exactly encourage him, either. Now, I could lose everything. And I did nothing."

I admitted the case was a hard one. Nevertheless, I saw how much the events in London had impacted her psychologically. I had run into her a week before the trip—she'd been excited, confident about her future, not this agitated, discouraged being, immobile in a hospital. Of course, the stabbing created much of her distress. On the other hand, she didn't seem as upset by that event as much as one might imagine. She explained that, terrible as it was, the stabbing had released her from the horrible burden she felt about leaving her husband.

"Finally, I can divorce him without guilt. Even my mother encouraged me to stay away from him. When he overturned furniture a couple of years ago, she told me to merely come over to their house when he got rowdy. Finally, she says it's okay to divorce him."

Her parents had expected her to put up with physical abuse? Perhaps, I pondered, it was due to her family's Catholic consciousness.

I did not see Caroline again for a few months. Then, after I'd just filed a quit claim deed in a more or less amicable dissolution, and I spotted her on the courthouse steps. "Good to see you're mobile."

She laughed. "I only hung out there for a week."

"How's school? And teaching?"

She frowned and glanced down at her feet. "I'm not teaching this semester. I'm working as a research assistant—writing a guide for students writing dissertations. Professor Darcy recommended me for the position. But I wanted to teach a class, too. He claimed the school wouldn't let me do both. I phoned the dean and found I could do both—the school didn't mind. When I told the professor, he said to stop by today, and he might have a class for me." She sighed. "Wouldn't you know it—today, when I had to go to court for the divorce. I just called the professor. He said another teacher took the class."

"That doesn't seem fair."

She smiled slightly. "I did get back at him, in a way. You remember that he'd claimed he knew too much about me? When I phoned from the hospital, I said merely that four inches of steel had gone through my chest and punctured my lung. After I returned to school, he was dying for me to confide in him, I could see it. He'd stand nearby when he'd see me. He'd step outside his office when he heard me in the lobby. I told a couple of other professors about the stabbing, but I never said a word about it to him. And he just kept waiting for me to tell him what I knew he already knew. That, at least, was comical."

Unfortunately, it probably wouldn't help her position in the department, I thought. I merely smiled. "Good luck."

For about five years, I lost touch with her. Then, one steamy summer afternoon, when the Midwest feared another flood, I ducked under awnings to avoid the shower as I strode down a sidewalk on the Country Club Plaza. She strolled from the other direction. No longer long and flowing, her hair swished just above her shoulders, and although she walked briskly, her step had lost its bounce. We greeted each other and stepped inside Emile's to share a cup of coffee. She'd been teaching part-time at two community colleges and free lancing for local newspapers.

"We need to keep in touch," she said. "Odd that I should run into you today, too, because I just discovered more tidbits about the professor."

I felt my eyebrows rise.

"A woman who teaches with me at one of the colleges also teaches at the university. Awhile back, he'd told her something about the London trip, said along the lines of 'losing your perspective when you're on an overnight flight with a woman.' Mind you, I told her nothing until after he'd made that comment, which she forwarded to me. But she also confided that he's sent other women away from the university—and that he came on to her, too. Anyway, between the community college and the university, she has more classes than she can handle this fall. So she asked the professor if I could take over hers at the university."

"So are you?"

She shook her head. "He told her, 'murky waters take a long time to clear.' I don't understand. It's been more than five years."

"Have you tried KU?"

She grimaced and shook her head again. "Too far. I drive Elizabeth to school and back. Besides, I hear the department there doesn't like to hire permanent teachers. It's odd. I've received wonderful peer evaluations, and my student evaluations are good. A male colleague said I just need to relocate. As if I could do that in a snap. It seems to be easier for men: They make the bucks. Plus, they can relocate—do whatever it takes to promote themselves in their careers. It isn't that simple for me. I own a house here. My daughter's in school here. I turned down a Fulbright because I can't uproot now. I can't just fly off and move across the country—at least, not on my salary or any salary most women make. Besides, even if I didn't, I might run into another situation, you know. Then what would I do?"

Solid as her arguments appeared, I sensed why she'd shied away from striving for a better position. Lack of confidence-lack of faith. Like a sugar maple caught with green leaves and sap flowing by an October snow that cracks its trunk, her once indomitable spirit seemed split, withered. I did not know how to help it flourish again, so I sipped my cappuccino and watched the rain splatter on car roofs, passersby, and asphalt. It seemed like it'd never let up.

Judith leaned back in her chair and inhaled deeply. Writing the piece had been exhilarating. Now she had to write the legal analysis and find a publisher.

Chapter Sixteen
Adam's Country Life

Adam had spent another day building a stable for the horses on Allie's farm. Her place wasn't a real farm. It was mainly acreage far south of Kansas City, beyond Cleveland, Missouri, where she housed three horses that her parents bought her. Her parents had bought the land, too, and the mobile home where Allie lived.

Of course, the pastures were mainly weeds because Allie didn't farm them. Instead, she played her flute, played with her dog, intermittently attended classes at Longview Community College, and rode her horses.

Her parents lived in an expensive house in Lakewood, a northern Lee's Summit lake community. They'd made money from various businesses, and now, they'd invested in oil commodities. So they were doing fine. Adam figured they'd bought the spot for Allie just to get her out of their home. Or perhaps Allie had pestered them so much for a place of her own, they finally gave in to her nagging. He didn't ask her about it.

She was a stocky girl, but still attractive. Her brown, silky hair had tinges of blonde in it, and her smooth, full lips and deep-set blue eyes that flickered often at some remark made her appear a bit sexy, too, Adam thought. She also laughed frequently, a deep, rich, full laugh. Adam especially liked that.

Although he'd noticed her around campus, he didn't really know her the first year he attended the college. In fact, he didn't know her name until they were in a music theory class together, that is, before the professor urged Allie to withdraw.

"You're not taking this seriously," the professor had said. "You'll hold the other students back."

Because this was this first formal music class that Adam had taken, Allie was abashed when he'd receive A's on tests where she'd ranked D's. She'd studied the flute and oboe since she was ten years old, in fifth grade. Here, this self-taught musician came along and blew away the curve for the rest of the students. So for a long time, she didn't like Adam—or so Adam believed.

Then, one day, each of them sat at a table in the cafeteria with a group of students who jabbering along about grades. She hadn't entered the conversation, Adam noticed. So he did.

"Hey—grades may be important to get scholarships," Adam said. "And maybe they'll help you transfer to a university. But they aren't true barometers of intelligence—or talent." He glanced at Allie, who smiled at him for the first time he'd recalled.

Later that day, she hung around the quadrangle where he and two other guys played a hectic game of hacky-sack. His martial arts training had helped his coordination, so he tended to win those informal competitions on campus. He'd won that one, then sat on

a concrete wall housing huge, tropical-looking flowers—
long, narrow red and yellow flowers with long golden
pistils.

"Wow," Allie said and sat next to him. "He's a
scholar—and an athlete, too."

Adam laughed. "Hardly. If you saw my high
school grades, you wouldn't say that."

"Really?"

"Yeah." He inhaled from a cigarette. "I only did
well in theory because I love it—I love composing, too.
I'm supposed to be getting a marketable degree here in
computer science. But man, I hate the math. And my
grades in it are nothing to brag about."

"So you don't like computers?"

"I love working on computers." Adam grinned.
"And I like programming them—started doing that with
a Trash 80 my mom bought at a pawn shop when I was
in middle school. I just hate studying the math in
computer science classes."

Allie smiled and patted his leg. "You're all right."
She drew one of her legs to her chest and wrapped her

arms around it. "So did you start playing using the *Susuki* method?" She smiled again, a broad smile that caused her nose to wrinkle.

Adam shook his head. "Actually, when I was a kid, I had about three piano lessons. Then, the teacher said it'd be better if I just went on doing what I was doing."

"Which was?"

"Just learning on my own. I think she didn't want to mess with me. I was a rowdy kid. I didn't have much patience with learning to read music."

Allie laughed again. She glanced away for a few minutes. Adam watched her watching the clouds which had rolled in from the west. Then she turned back to him. "Say, do you like to ride?"

"Ride what?"

She laughed again. "Horses, of course."

"I used to ride almost every day when we lived in the mountains by Breckenridge." Adam shrugged. "It was fun."

"I have three horses. We can ride 'em any time."

"Sounds like fun. I haven't been on one for awhile, but I hear it's like riding a bicycle." He grinned and hoped she got the joke.

She smiled. "Sorta. Except bicycles don't have minds of their own. If you don't have any more classes today, we could go there now. It's about forty minutes away."

So Adam followed her for what seemed like forever south to her farm. They spent an hour on the horses, riding them through fields of long grasses, over hills and bluffs, then back around to her trailer. After they'd unsaddled and brushed the horses, they headed inside. Unfortunately, one of Allie's hounds didn't like Adam. He growled with each step Adam made toward the door.

"Down, Bruiser, down—he's been nasty lately. I don't know what his problem is."

"How old is he?"

"I dunno. At least ten." Allie tried patting the dog on the head. He still growled, so she shooed him away. Hanging his head, he shuffled off to a doghouse under a nearby elm. There, head still down, he circled a food dish, then finally, lay down inside the house.

"Maybe he's losing his sight. A friend of my mom's had a dog that became irritable once she couldn't see anymore." He shrugged and shook a cigarette from his pack. "I mean, dogs can't see that well anyway. But this dog got downright nasty—awoke from a dream I guess and snapped at my sister when she was only five."

"Was she teasing him?"

"No. The dog just awoke and made a bee-line for her—for no apparent reason. And then she bit her and broke the skin."

"So what happened to the dog?"

"My mom's friend put her down." He flicked an ash onto the gravel drive. "The dog was old, though. So my mom's friend knew it was time. I think the dog was about thirteen."

Suddenly, a flock of geese flew overhead. They squawked and honked, then in a V-formation, they began circling the small pound lying about twenty yards away from Allie's house.

Adam watched them land and splash, then start skittering into the water. He loved their free attitude. "Cool," he said and cuffed one of Allie's arms. "You really do live in the country."

Chapter Seventeen
Mick Clues in Judith

Mick stared out the living room window and couldn't believe what he saw—there, in the middle of the street, in front of a school bus yet, Jenny lifted her over-sized T-shirt and flashed the children. It seemed she wore nothing underneath it, and Mick saw her large breasts bob like water balloons. "Judith—Judith, come here! You've got to see this!"

But by the time Judith made it down stairs, a woman had run out from the house next door to Jenny's and wrapped the crazy woman in a bathrobe. All Judith saw was the backs of the two of them as they shuffled back into Jenny's bungalow.

"What?" Judith rubbed her eyes then stretched her arms above her head. He liked the way she looked with her hair mussed and sleepy-eyed. He thought she looked sexy. And he liked the way she smelled in the mornings, kind of like cream. It seemed she never had morning breath, either. She yawned then tugged back the curtain and looked outside. "Is that Jenny? What's she doing? Whassup?"

Mick laughed so hard he had to plop into a chair. "Jenny just flashed that school bus. She lifted up her shirt and I saw her breasts. I don't think she wore underpants, either. But I'm not sure. I was so shocked, I forgot to look."

"Oh, yeah, I bet."

"Oh, c'mon. It was Jenny. She looks like a bull-dog and her boobs sag."

She tried to hold her mouth firm, but Mick could see the corners of her lips trembled as she tried to keep from grinning. Finally, she fell into laughter. Then she seemed to force her face into a serious pose. "You know, we shouldn't laugh. The poor thing went off her meds, and now she's in her manic phase. And her love life hasn't been going all that well." Judith squinted and looked sternly at Mick. "Did I tell you her boyfriend, that guy Eddy, got beat up?"

He shook his head. "You're kidding?" Rod and George hadn't beat up Eddy after the party, as Mick had initially thought they did. Instead, they'd lured him into Rod's car with promises of free pot, took him for a ride about a mile east, gave him a pat-down, found Judith's wallet, then yelled at him and dumped him in a bar's parking lot along Troost Avenue. Afterwards, Rod and George stopped at a liquor store, picked up a twelve-pack and a bottle of wine, and brought them back to the party. They'd said nothing to anyone but Mick. Instead, they acted as if they'd gone on a booze run. So Mick was curious about what Judith had discovered. "So when did this happen?"

"Some time after our party. Jenny wasn't sure why Eddy left, and he couldn't remember much. He said he got into a car with a couple of guys who gave him a ride somewhere near Troost. They left him and drove on. So a gang of teenagers came across Eddy passed out on the asphalt, and they started kicking him. Hurt him."

"So is he still living there?"

"I believe Jenny kicked him out for dumping her at our party—along with all the other slimy things he'd done."

"Like stealing your checkbook."

"What?" She glared at him, then wrinkled her forehead. "I thought Rod and George found it by bushes next to the porch. I thought maybe I'd left it on the ledge and it fell off of it."

"Nawh." Mick shook his head. "They figured it was him. So they frisked him before he left. He was so loaded, he didn't know what was happening. But they found your checkbook and got it back to you. Plus, they didn't want you to get upset at anyone that night. They didn't want to ruin your party. They're good guys that way. Good people."

She raised her eyebrows. "At least, my money was all there."

"It wouldn't have been if it weren't for Rod and

George." Mick started whistling "Yankee Doodle" and headed back toward the kitchen. Finally, his friends stood in good stead with his wife, at least for now. And hers looked mighty silly. He chuckled to himself. *Sometimes you eat the bear, and sometimes the bear eats you*, Uncle Todd used to say. And yes, today that proved true. Now, he wished she'd tell her kids about this. Neither one of them showed him enough respect. And that Krystal—there had to be some way he could control her. He opened the refrigerator and pulled out a beer. After all, it was almost noon and he had the day off. He needed to celebrate a little. He hadn't had a drink all week, not since the party last Saturday. He'd just screwed off the lid and downed a gulp when the phone rang. It was Sandy, a new shift manager.

"Mick, Carla hasn't showed. I tried her cell phone but no answer. Man, we're getting' slammed, and we're really short—"

"Umm. You tried Rick?"

"He's gone to Columbia—got to pick up his brother."

Mick hadn't been off for six days. He'd even worked half a shift the day of the party—usually his day off since he became general manager—because one of the guys caught some virus. In fact, he'd taken today, Wednesday, off to make up for working that day and part of Sunday. He frowned. Part of why he agreed to the heavy burden of running the largest Haven in the region was to get weekends off.

"You tried Rod?"

"He's supposed to come in at eleven."

"Call him and tell him I want him there now. And have him call me when he arrives."

If Rod did this, Mick swore he'd give him a raise. He wasn't sure how, but he thought he would promote him to shift manager, too. The kid *was* management material. And he'd proved himself in more ways than one. Besides, he couldn't go in today—not with beer on his breath. He might like to party, but he didn't want it to interfere with his job, especially since he was finally moving up again. He hadn't made this much money since he'd worked for McDonald's a decade ago. That company had sent him to Hamburger U, where he'd received some of the best management training in the world. Fortune 500 companies sent trainees to Hamburger U. So Mick was proud of that degree, even if it wasn't a bachelor's or something snazzy.

Now after straggling at the bottom of the Haven's empire, he was once again climbing his way back to the top. And he'd need good men behind him, men he could lift up with him, men like Rod and maybe, George. So now, Rod would have to do what he did—come in whenever the boss calls, clean up messes, go above and beyond what's asked. And smile-smile-smile at those customers. Give them extra fries, give them an extra soda here and there, keep them happy and calling the 800 number to compliment you and your restaurant. Yes, he knew the game. And finally, once more, he had the chance to play it, if he could just keep up his energy, his drive. He had to admit that the restaurant business was a young man's business. At least, until you owned your own place. But he knew Judith wouldn't invest her savings into one. He didn't understand why she needed that nest egg—always throwing money into savings. The woman needed to live, to learn to take risks with investments. That's the only way you could have a big payoff. But she was a conservative investor who only trusted banks.

Finally, after spending nearly every penny he made on partying or women, he'd started an account of his own now. He hadn't told Judith about it, either. Not that she'd care. She always urged him to save money. But he knew she wouldn't be happy if he saved it then sank it into buying a restaurant, especially if he had none left once he did.

Yet, last week, when one of the district managers from the Haven in Mexico had called him about joining in a partnership to form a new restaurant, Mick liked the idea. When he mentioned it to Judith, she didn't become angry—merely said they didn't have that much dough. But somehow, someway, Mick would come up with the dough. He knew he could. And maybe, just maybe, once he reaped lots of dough, this family would respect him for a change, just maybe they would.

Still, he couldn't imagine where to find that much money or how long it would take him to save it. He just couldn't save the way Judith did.

He swigged another gulp of beer. It was cool and bittersweet, just the way he liked it.

Chapter Eighteen
Adam Investigates

"Great musicality is a higher revelation than wisdom and philosophy." Reading this quotation from Ludwig Van Beethoven during his music theory class had empowered Adam. Finally, he'd found something that made him feel worthwhile. Even if Joe had turned out to be a jerk, Adam was glad the man had encouraged him about composing. It gave Adam hope. Today, he thought about the quote again when he blinked open his eyes. He yawned, and heard a voice from the front room.

Allie's television was tuned into *Channel 9 News*, which spieled warnings from the *New England Journal of Medicine* about CAT scans. News reporter Charles

Euwalt was interviewing a local M.D. for his take on the findings. Having one CAT scan wasn't dangerous, the M.D. explained. But *The Journal* article outlined studies that showed future effects of numerous CAT scans upon the population. It speculated that the increased use of the scans could cause up to two percent of cancers within the next two decades.

"CAT scans send out one hundred to two hundred times more radiation than a simple X-ray," Euwalt said. "The article says sometimes CAT scans are necessary, but many doctors are exposing 20 million adults and one million children to high doses of radiation needlessly. Doctor, why do you think this is?"

"They've so revolutionized diagnosis that doctors have over-prescribed them," the M.D. replied. "They've been instrumental in locating brain tumors early on. So it's easy to see how it happened. But doctors shouldn't just prescribe them to anyone who comes in with a headache." The doctor cleared his throat. "And some of the doctors have been sending patients to CAT scan facilities that they own. The AMA has been looking into this—believes it's unethical." Adam frowned. Then, he blinked again and looked around for Allie. He heard no noise in the bath room or kitchen, only the blaring television. Apparently, she'd gone outside.

Now the TV rattled on about the Dow being up well over 13,000 points—the best rally in more than two years. "Went up more than one hundred points the first two hours of trading," some commentator said. The commentator attributed the rally to a three dollar a barrel drop in oil prices.

Hearing oil had dropped caught Adam's attention. Maybe gas would fall finally, too, he thought. With that, he pulled himself up into a cross-legged sitting position. He looked at his watch. It was three p.m. "Shit," he said. "Missed my math class." It was the third time this semester, and it was only the end of October. He couldn't miss another one, or his grade would be docked. Even if he didn't like the class, he didn't want to take any chances. Skipping too many classes in high school had taught him that wasn't a smart plan. Neither was skipping out on homework, which, so far, he hadn't done at the community college. In fact, because Krystal's parent-teacher conferences at her grade school and Adam's were at the same time on the same day, Mick had gone to talk with Adam's teachers. His economics instructor had informed Mick that Adam received the highest grade on the final in all five of the classes he taught. Nevertheless, Adam would receive only a C because the kid wouldn't do his daily homework. When Mick had confronted Adam about it, he'd shrugged.

"I only got that high of a grade because I read the assignments the night before the test," he'd replied then shrugged again. "So the information was still fresh in my mind."

Mick had said nothing and as usual, shook his head. In fact, the rolled eyes and shaking head seemed to be Mick's main responses to Adam. Nevertheless, Adam appreciated Mick meeting with his teachers. In fact, it'd rather surprised him because Mick wouldn't let Adam call him "Dad." "I'm your friend," he said the first time Adam tried the address. "Not your father." Then he'd cleared his throat and frowned. "And I hope my own kids won't call anyone else 'Dad.'" So Adam didn't call him that again.

His performance in the economics class was typical to Adam's style of learning. The truth was, except when it involved practicing scales or reading a musical staff, Adam considered daily exercises to be "busy work" and a waste of his time. He'd tried to be diligent. He'd tried to major in a "marketable" field. But it was no use. He just couldn't continue the façade. And he wasn't sure how he'd break it to his mother and to his grandmother, who helped fund his education, that no way did he want to major in computer programming. He'd either major in music or screw it—he wouldn't go to college, period.

The trailer door banged, and Allie stepped inside. "Hey, Sleepyhead. What's up?" She smiled at him then brushed what looked like hayseed off her jeans and headed toward the kitchen.

"Wish you would've awakened me," Adam yawned again. "I missed my math class. I can't afford to do that again."

"Why don't you drop the stupid class?" she called from the kitchen as she opened the refrigerator, pulled out a bottle of orange juice, swigged a gulp from it, and stuck it back on the shelf. "You hate it, and I thought you already decided you weren't going to do the computer science major."

"I know. But I should probably finish the class anyway." Adam shook and yanked on his slacks. "My mom and grandma already paid for the class. It wouldn't be fair to them."

"Maybe you could get some of your tuition refunded."

He shook his head. "Too late in the semester. It's already mid-term."

"It won't do them any good either if you won't use it for a degree." She shrugged. "Besides, it isn't like community college hours cost what the university's do."

"True." Adam clicked his belt. "But the class might transfer for a requirement at the university. And if I screw up, I doubt they'll help me get through the conservatory."

"You never know." She smiled again. "Parents worry. You can get by with screwing up more than you think. Especially if you convince them you've turned over a new leaf—and that you need their help to get your life back on track. You know the lines."

It dawned on him then that Allie might be terribly manipulative. He'd have to watch her, he decided, keep an eye out for himself. He liked her quite a bit, but he couldn't have her ruin his life. Quickly, he threw on his shirt and downed a glass of water. He kissed her on the cheek then jiggled his keys, tossed them in the air and caught them.

"Gotta get home," he said. "Mom's expecting me by four-thirty."

"Really?" She tilted her head to one side and squinted.

"Don't be like that." He pecked her on the cheek again and flew out the door. It was a beautiful day. Perhaps he'd go for a walk once he got back to his neighborhood. It was a great place for walking, better even than the country. Besides, he liked the way his mother's house generally smelled of chocolate chip cookies, which she baked almost daily.

Later that night, Adam was glad he went home. Judith had tuned in the PBS station to the second Eric Clapton Crossroads Guitar Festival. This time, it was in Chicago. Adam recorded it and he and Mick played air guitar with Johnny Winter, Blind Faith, Jeff Beck, and, of course, Clapton. Then Clapton performed some Blind Faith tunes with Steve Winwood. Adam especially liked the way Jeff Beck fused rock and jazz. He'd been trying to fuse classical music with rock. His friends and his mother liked it, but he still hadn't perfected it. So he hadn't wanted to distribute CDs of the piece, not yet. Somehow, he couldn't make his mother comprehend this, either.

"Make me a tape," Judith had demanded again and again, "or burn me a CD. I want to play this in my car. Or at least, have a record of it before you decide you don't like it anymore and dump it." That was the problem—after he'd cut a track, he'd like it at first. Then, he'd hear all the flaws and wouldn't want anyone else to hear the piece. It seemed he couldn't get anything to be absolutely perfect, and music had to be absolutely perfect. Or it just didn't work.

Tonight, the concert went on for more than two hours. It was a nice treat, and even though Mick drank so much he became obnoxious, the evening went pretty well. Adam would study the videotape they'd made of the show and perhaps he'd learn something from Beck, Clapton, and Winwood, even if he didn't play the guitar. There was a technique for merging that they'd conquered, though. He was determined to conquer it, too.

Chapter Nineteen
Judith's Fear and Loathing

The night after Judith made reservations for a trip to Vegas so she and Mick could enjoy a short vacation, she couldn't get to sleep. She was uncertain about the trip, but she hoped perhaps it could help get them back together. Finally, she dozed off, but she had a strange dream.

In the dream, amid smells of Caesar's Ferentina perfume, one she often bought, she sat at a row of poker machines, dropping in quarters as in the old days. Then, she punched three buttons to hold a pair of kings and an ace on the Draw Poker game, the only one letting her get ahead tonight. Another ace popped up. She felt herself grow warm and smiled. Red letters flashed on the screen to congratulate her three-credit win, then beckoned her to vie with the dealer—high card on draw, double or nothing. In the dream, she calculated whether the dealer would pull a high one this time, then went for it. The machine dealt the dealer a one-eyed Jack.

"Shoot." She'd said then shoved her long hair back from her cheeks and smoothed the skirt on her denim dress that flowed like a nightgown around her legs. Judith actually owned a denim dress like that one. Often, she wore it to relax, which she wanted to do in the dream. She didn't want to think about studying for law school and she'd wanted to get away from Mick. She sighed at the Jack. Apparently, she'd miscalculated the machine's patterns. It figured a one-eyed Jack would pop up. The card reminded her of Mick. He might not be one-eyed, but she could see how his vision emulated a blind man's. Any more, it seemed that to him, money, booze, and dope were all. And yes, of course, he talked constantly about the Haven.

She punched the second card from the right. A

queen. In her dream, she felt lucky, certainly luckier than she she'd felt earlier in the suite. In fact, since she'd come downstairs, she'd been trying to ignore the lyrics pulsing through Caesar's PA system: "I was meant for you, and you were meant for me." They, too, reminded her of Mick, and she was unsure why. Maybe those words had been true six years ago, but no more. In fact, she mainly came downstairs to get away from him. She liked Vegas and all its glitz, but she wasn't much of a gambler. So she'd play Draw Poker till she quit winning. Then, maybe she could sleep.

She pressed the "Play one credit" button again and glanced at the casino entrance. A bald man with deep-set, hooded eyes—a poet's or a convict's eyes, large ears, and a full white beard lumbered into the room. Wearing a railroad engineer's striped overalls, he stood out in Caesar's like a hog at high tea. He also seemed oddly familiar.

After she watched him amble into the quarter-machine area, it dawned on her that she'd seen him a long, long time ago. He was the farmer who had once approached her in the field when she'd run away from home. She was 13 then. Or were the late night and neon lights playing tricks on her? She blinked. No, he was the one, all right. But even with his brown, withered cheeks and crow's feet, he looked no older than he had that day thirty years ago.

She couldn't recall precisely why she'd run away, except she'd had a spat with her mother. More than anything, she remembered crying while she jaunted on a highway shoulder, the traffic's roar reverberating in her head. In fact, the traffic's loud moans had scared her—forced her off the road. For the first time, she feared dying. She'd wandered through a pasture and had climbed almost over a fence rimmed with barbed wire. Then the fencing tore loose, and she fell. The barbed wire scraped her knees, tore runs in her hose. Her legs became a bloody mess of nylon interwoven with flesh. When she'd struggled to stand and try the fence again, the white-haired man had appeared about fifteen feet away. He'd frightened her.

"You all right?" he'd asked in a gruff voice. An

expression in his eyes had scared her, too. She'd stared at him a second then bolted the other direction, sprinting over clumps of grass and dirt clods, leaping and running as fast as she could. Long, prickly weeds stung her legs, but still she ran across a pasture and back to the highway. At least, that was all she remembered. At times, though, especially when she'd read tracts about repressed events, she wondered if more had happened and she'd blocked it out. If so, she'd succeeded at blocking any memories of a sexual act. Nevertheless, it remained strange that after thirty years, the scene still loomed in her mind, like some destiny she wanted to avoid but couldn't.

And here, out of nowhere, the man re-appeared.

He seemed to survey the room as if he were looking for someone. Then he looked toward Judith. She looked back at the Draw Poker table and pressed the deal button. She'd moved her stare before his eyes caught it but felt his gaze on her. Her checks reddened. She was glad she'd missed his stare because she feared his eyes would flicker with the bestial fire she'd seen in them when she was child. She hated the glimmer of lust anymore, even in Mick. It led to rough sex—all passion, no tenderness—no longer to gentle kisses and soft caresses. And she wished the white-bearded man would leave the room. Of course, he didn't. Instead, he ambled over to the machine next to hers.

Judith sighed. She wanted nothing to do with the man. She loved Mick, even though their marriage had become a typical alcoholic union. This afternoon, he'd gulped the half-100 proof Bacardi, half-Coke concoction he'd been guzzling since 10 a.m., then growled, "Get a real job!" His breath reeked, and brown rimmed the edges of his teeth, giving him a sinister look. A black vein throbbed on his forehead. His eyes, once glittery, had become duller and duller. "Forty-three years old and how far you gotten? You're a loser—teaching part-time while you go to school—and you've published a tiny book—but nothing big time! Your writing's just a fantasy! A fairytale! And this law school thing just costs more than it's worth."

"I'm paying for it out of my savings!" She turned

from him and stared at the mirror. Dark circles rimmed her eyes. But her writing and teaching had improved, she knew it. Obviously, Mick didn't. Maybe his lack of faith in her had slowed her success after they married. That's why she'd enrolled in law school, to have something as backup while she continued writing, something that paid better than teaching. He just didn't get it. "Look—I tried slaving in an office for the big bucks. It didn't work. I'm an artist. And if I become a lawyer, I can make good money while I continue to write." She spoke the words to his reflection then ducked when he jerked up from the bed. "You touch me, and I'll call the police."

"I ain't goin' to hit you." He sat on the bed. "But don't you ask for alimony—blood will splatter."

Shortly after supper time, he'd passed out. In the dream, just as in waking hours anymore, she wasn't sure what to do about Mick. She'd known he was a drinker when they married, but when he'd claimed he found Jesus, she'd believed him. She was there—it'd seemed so real. Besides, she'd seen drunks saved from the bottle that way. She figured it'd be only a matter of time till Mick saw the light. Yet after six years, the light he saw most often came from the fridge when he grabbed another Budweiser. It seemed he'd never change. So she'd learned to make the best of his drunkenness again and again.

Suddenly, the dream went to a scene where she strolled down the strip and clicked snapshots. Like singing, shooting photos gave her a sense of control. She focused the camera on red, blue, and beige casinos—a castle, a Tudor, and neoclassical buildings like Caesars and the Monte Carlo. It helped her relax.

Then the dream returned her to the casino where she sat paying poker. Other images from the past six months appeared. Even in her dream, they rattled her— the long, black hairs on her pillow after she'd attended a two-week seminar out-of-town. The low, breathy voice from someone named "Linda" on the answering machine a month later. "Linda" had said she loved Mick and added he'd left some "things" at her place. (Mick claimed it was a wrong number, but Judith truly didn't know what to believe.) The maroon lipstick on Mick's shirt tail. Judith never wore that color. Nonetheless, she preferred Mick's infidelities and yeasty smell to the rancid scent of the white-haired man who now stood next to her.

"Any luck?" the man asked. From a sideward glance, she noted he didn't smile, and the white hairs in his nose were unclipped.

"A little." Judith focused again on the machine. She wondered if her fear lured strange men to her. Supposedly, dogs would attack when they smelled a human's fear. Perhaps some men responded in kind. Perhaps then, the rancid scent was hers. But she didn't think so. Earlier, she'd smelled of Ferentina, she was sure of it. And she couldn't shake the old geezer. It seemed another hour passed while the old guy hung around her with a dog's tenacity. What was odd, too, was that it seemed he'd plunked only one quarter into the machine. Maybe he was a pro, and his attire a ruse.

Nonetheless, he frightened her. Although she was winning, she cashed out and scooped up the coins.

"Going so soon?"

She caught herself biting her lip. "Getting late."

"But you've been winning."

"Yeah. Best to leave before my luck runs out."

"Maybe it won't now."

She looked at him. He grinned, pulled an ace of spades seemingly from the air, and tossed it onto her machine. So the old guy was a magician. Maybe he worked in the Caesars Magical Empire show.

"Try one more deal." He grinned again, picked out a quarter—again from the air—and dropped it into Judith's machine. She stared at him longer this time and noticed he resembled her grandfather. But her grandfather had deep eyes with pupils like oceans. This man's pupils were flat—like black shields hiding something. Pupils like those she'd seen in other magicians. No, his eyes weren't a poet's at all. He nodded toward the machine, and something about his expression coerced her to punch the deal button. She watched the machine deal. A straight flush. The machine dinged like crazy and awarded her 8,000 credits. Eight thousand quarters—$2,000. She felt her eyes widen. She shook her head then laughed. "But how? I only played one credit. You're supposed to play five to win that much."

The old man said nothing but grinned again.

"The setting on the machine must be off." She felt herself grin again. "I'll be sure to try it tomorrow night."

"No, you won't."

His words unnerved her. She pressed the cash out button. Thousands of quarters began clanging into the changer. Then, it stopped. "How rude of me." She turned to the old man. "This win's yours."

"No. It's yours. Keep the first quarter, too. It might be lucky."

She scooped up quarters, then glanced again at the old man. His face held no expression, but he watched her the way a hunter watches a squirrel or rabbit before moving in. Perhaps he was an eccentric casino owner who dressed like a farmer, then wooed women this way.

"It's a beautiful night—seventy degrees, faint wind, moonlight dancing over the mountains. Does a ride in a convertible—a black, Jaguar X-16—suit you?"

"Oh—I couldn't do that." Judith's arms quivered. She kept her eyes on the quarters. Of course, he was coming onto her. Maybe he was a rich rancher. Often they dressed strangely. Still, she couldn't let him get too close—he scared her too much.

"Are you afraid your husband would mind? He shouldn't. He doesn't enjoy life anymore—the sweetness of romance, the gentle quirks of jealousy, the visions of future glory. He hates it, doesn't he?"

Judith felt herself squint. It seemed his rancid smell grew strong. She stepped back, shivered, and crossed her arms. "How do you know I'm married?"

The man grinned and nodded at her left hand. "Your ring. And how do I know your husband has lost his lust for life? Pure reasoning. He's here at the nation's playground with a beautiful wife—who isn't a shrew—and he doesn't join her or entice her to spend the evening with him."

"How do you know he isn't in the casino playing another machine?"

"Because you'd glance around for him every now and then. You'd go to his machine, nuzzle up to him. Or he'd come to yours."

Judith sighed and admitted to herself that her situation was likely more obvious than she'd supposed. Besides, the man had given her two thousand dollars. Perhaps she owed him some time. "I'll buy you a drink, if you like."

"I'm surprised you drink."

She shrugged. "Just now and then."

"I mean, with all the havoc it's caused you."

She glared at him, looking over his frayed overalls and pointed teeth. How did he know? Was he some sort of psychic? She'd heard some magicians were. His grin seemed smug now, taunting. Then, again, he'd probably seen her hanging out here, and maybe he saw Mick getting soused. Still, it made her uneasy, too, to think, the old man had been stalking her.

"I suppose you see that a lot around here."

He nodded.

After a coin person came to give Judith the rest of her win and she exchanged the coins for cash, she and the old man sat in a bar where she'd watched some good acts the past two years. But now, no band performed. The equipment remained on stage, looking lifeless as tree branches in winter. The empty stage made her feel melancholic, the way she always felt after a gig she attended alone, the way she felt when the audience dispersed, when maybe one musician would hang out and share a drink with her. And many times, she sat by herself to chill out before she returned to her room.

That night, the bar's PA system now played the Stones' "I Can't Get No Satisfaction." But Heart's "Dog and Butterfly" lyrics and riffs from the other system—or maybe they were just in her mind—vied with the Stones' song. She stared at the yellow, floral wallpaper behind the bar till one brown lily blurred into another one. This had become her life. Mick's insecurities had blended into her psyche. He'd been feeling suicidal the last three months, he said so today. So had she. Until tonight in her dream. She glanced at her strange companion. "I've been so rude. I've forgotten to thank you for encouraging me. Uh, I don't know your name, either."

He smiled grimly. "Lucien."

"French?"

"Latin. Ancient. Like me."

"Oh, no. I wouldn't say—"

"You needn't. It's true."

She felt sorry for him. "We all grow old. And it beats the alternative—"

"Yes, the alternative."

His tone sent chills through her arms again. He didn't sound sad or even wistful. In fact, his tone sounded as if he'd experienced death frequently. She sipped her Bloody Mary. He didn't drink his Black Russian, but stirred it, then leaned back and pulled something from the air again. He placed it on the table. It was a broach—an ivory cameo on black onyx, an antique. It reminded Judith of a broach her grandmother once owned. But it'd been lost years ago. No one could find it after the old woman had died.

Judith remembered it because her mother had made such a fuss—supposedly, her grandmother had promised it to her mother. The finely carved ivory was no doubt valuable.

"You like it?"

"Of course."

"It's yours."

"No. It isn't." Judith stood and looked toward the elevators leading to her room. "Look. You're a very nice man. But I can't take gifts from you. I don't know you."

He squinted. "I believe you know me more than you realize."

She looked at him and kept shivering. Perhaps he truly was the man she'd seen so long ago. If so, she didn't care. He'd scared her then, and he scared her now. She didn't need to put up with this malarkey any more. She backed away from the table. "You're a swell fellow. And you've probably just lost someone dear to you. But I must go now."

"You don't understand. I can't leave here alone tonight."

"Look. I understand what it's like to be lonely. But I must go back to my room. You've got the wrong person."

He smiled grimly again. "Yes. Perhaps I do."

She turned and almost fled to the elevator. She'd thought about giving him the money she'd won with his quarter. But she didn't want to face him again. Tomorrow, she'd talk to the manager. Maybe someone knew who he was. Maybe she'd leave it in an envelope for him.

She flashed her door card to the security man, punched an up arrow, and crossed her arms. She stepped behind the guard so the old man at the table couldn't see her. Usually this late at night—or early in the morning—the elevators moved quickly. Of course, they didn't now. It seemed all of them were stuck on some floor above. She watched the floors light, but all the elevators kept stopping on a floor or two above the casino. She glanced back once toward the bar. At least, the old guy hadn't followed her. Then, she looked at the table she'd shared with him. He'd left. She scanned the room. Perhaps he was behind a video or slot machine. Perhaps he planned to follow her to her room. Finally, an elevator arrived. She was happy to find it empty. She pressed the button for the thirteenth floor and sighed.

Judith remained apprehensive when she arrived on her floor. She listened for footsteps in the corridor before she left the landing and scanned the doorways and fire escape exits. She wondered if Mick had awakened. She wanted to tell him about this strange adventure, certainly about the win, but she decided she'd better not. He'd rail at her for taking up with the stranger, and he'd insist upon keeping the money. And she still might leave it in an envelope for the old man. She began to feel sorry for the old guy now that he wasn't around to frighten her. She glanced down the corridor. Then, she gasped: she thought she saw the old man dart from some room at the end and out the fire escape. She shook her head and glanced at her watch. It was almost four a.m.

Obviously, her fatigue had caused hallucinations. Nonetheless, she glanced to each side when she slid in her card to unlock the door. When it slammed, she was surprised Mick didn't stir. Oddly enough, he didn't snore, either. Most nights after a binge, he snored so loudly, she'd hear him across the hall. But tonight, he lay silent, motionless on the bed, arms sprawled. One hand dangled over the side just a few inches from the now empty fifth stuck in a gummy ring on the coffee table. Another empty fifth had rolled under an end table. She frowned, shivered, undressed as silently as possible, and slipped into the other bed.

In her dream, she slept in the next morning and was surprised Mick still lay silent. She glanced at the clock. It was 12:35 p.m. Usually, after a day of drinking, Mick would spring out of bed the next morning at seven. She pulled herself up, crossed her legs, and glanced at him. "Wake up. Today will be better."

He didn't budge. She noticed that he lay in the exact position he had when she'd come into the room. "Mick. Boy, you tied one on. But time to get up."

He still didn't stir. She squinted. His chest didn't move, either. She glared at him, then sprang toward

him, clutched one of his wrists, and drew it to her chest.
No pulse. She stared at him and held his wrist awhile
before she folded it to his torso. She picked up the
receiver to dial the front desk and clutched the phone a
long, long time.

In fact, when she awoke, Judith still felt the cold,
hard plastic receiver in her hand. She still shivered, too,
and she glanced over at Mick. He was definitely alive.
His hairy chest rose and fell in its usual systolic, diastolic
rhythms while he snored as loudly as ever. She slipped
out of the bed and hurried downstairs and into the
kitchen.

She turned on the fluorescent light, which glared
on the table where she'd left the papers containing the
details of her trip—confirmation and phone numbers,
dates and times. Staring at her hastily written, sprawling
notes, she wondered if she should call and cancel it. But
she wasn't sure the airlines or Caesar's would refund her
money. Perhaps she was silly, she thought. Yet, surreal
as it was, something about the dream seemed so real, the
images of the lights, the smells, and the strange, old man

seemed to cut deeply into her. Indeed, the man had resembled a farmer who'd approached her when she was thirteen. She'd had a fight with her mother, after which she'd started to run away. Yes, that memory was real. So were the memories about the strange phone calls from some woman named "Linda." Even though Mick had denied knowing her, just as he had in the dream, Judith didn't completely trust him.

She picked up her coffee mug decorated with large letters spelling "Mom" and slipped it into the microwave. With the amount of cream she drank in her coffee, it and a cigarette often helped her sleep. Yes, despite what all the women's magazines and health journals reiterated, the *café au lait* and cigarette worked for her, better than anything.

She glanced around the kitchen. *Why did everything look more cluttered than usual—the papers on the table, the dish towels hanging on the range handle, the large, wooden salt and pepper shakers next to a figurine that Adam had bought her three Christmases before?* She wondered. It seemed that no matter how many papers she tossed, no matter how many dresses, slacks, or sweaters she gave away, ten times the amount somehow re-filled her house. At times, she worried that she'd become some hoarder, like the strange women who'd appeared on *Oprah*. After living in a 3,000 square foot house for thirty-five years, the gray-haired, chubby woman who looked like a quintessential grandmother, had filled it with sixteen tons of trash. Yes, the Oprah team weighed it, probably to embarrass the woman more than the situation already embarrassed her. Plus, once the Oprah team sorted out all the marketable goods—racks of clothing the woman never wore, boxes of children's toys and baby clothes, all unused, kitchen bowls and toasters, and on and on—the team held a garage sale that reaped merely $2,000. The woman had likely spent more than five times that on the merchandise. Judith chuckled when she thought about it again. America. *Capitalism. Capitalism on steroids.* She certainly wasn't a socialist, but she wondered how the system could keep expanding and expanding—like some huge balloon, growing and growing—it was the very nature of capitalism—how could it continue without eventually exploding? Where was all this going anyway? At times, she wondered how she could simplify her life— get rid of so much unnecessary stuff. But each time she tried to do so, it seemed the mail brought in more than she'd tossed. *Again and again, it was always the same, such a dreary routine.*

Then Judith wondered what sort of life she'd woven for herself anyway. She'd built an arsenal of credentials—five years working as a newspaper reporter and magazine editor, an MA, nearly a PhD, and now a JD? *Why? For what? Was it just to acquire a marketable degree so she could earn decent money or to prove to herself she was smart, that she wasn't like most visitors on Oprah, Dr. Phil or The Jerry Springer Show?*

She sighed, slipped into a chair at the kitchen table, lit a cigarette and sipped her coffee. She thought about turning on *Charlie Rose*, but no—it was far too late. And tonight, she couldn't take *Jimmy Kimmel*. She was sick of television shows and of poring over law texts.

More than anything, she wanted more time to read a good novel. One of her colleagues at the university had written, *Hello I Must Be Going*, an engaging novel written from the point of view of a young girl whose father had shot himself. Judith had read more than two hundred pages of the three hundred page book and felt guilty that she hadn't finished it yet. *No time, no time, no time.* And tonight, if she picked up the novel, she'd not put it down for more than an hour. She needed to return to sleep before then. She glanced around the room again then took her Bible from the shelf and opened it to wherever the pages fell. "Seek ye first the kingdom of God and His righteousness. Then, all these things will be added unto you." Luke 12: 31.

The kingdom of God—how, oh *how*, could she stay focused on that? Didn't God's kingdom comprise *agapè* love, generosity, kindness, compassion, forgiveness, and God's eternal mercy and grace? Striving to maintain God's kingdom was the answer, she knew it.

On the other hand, in this world, how could she maintain such a consciousness when she felt like crying almost every day, when she felt so ripped off by this insane society with its greedy people shoving around kind people, people who didn't put money or power above integrity? How could she seek that sublime kingdom when she couldn't even get her husband to join her in prayer, to unite with her to focus on God's kingdom? Indeed, her marriage had been a sacrifice at the altar as surely as Abraham's had been. Now, it remained a mystery to her, how she could solve this problem with Mick. She rose and re-filled her cup of coffee, slid it into the microwave, and waited for the ding.

Suddenly, her new cat, Christine, meandered into the kitchen, sat beside her milk bowl, and stared at Judith. "Meow," she said peevishly and blinked.

"You stinker." Judith shook her head then arose and opened the refrigerator. "You aren't supposed to have milk until morning. But I guess it's morning to you."

She trickled some milk into the cat's dish. Christine sniffed at the bowl, hesitated a few seconds, then finally lapped the milk quickly. Judith watched the cat and chuckled. Finally, she re-read the scripture again, inhaled a deep breath and tried to relax. If she were lucky, she'd return to sleep in less than thirty minutes. Then she flipped through the Bible, stopping here and there to read a verse that strengthened her, and prayed until tears rolled down her cheeks.

Chapter Twenty
Mick's Fear and Loathing

Lately, Mick had suffered uneasy dreams, too. In them, he kept returning to scenes from his time in the service. Mick was a helicopter mechanic, but he did more than work on the engines. Lucky enough to do only one Viet Nam tour, Mick was posted in Alaska instead of the frontlines. Still, he suffered when he saw choppers arrive with gruesome scenes inside them—blood and guts splattered on walls as if they were pieces of hamburger—spaghetti or lasagna, and every so often, here and there, he found a detached finger or a huge chunk of flesh. And the smells—he knew he'd never shake the rank smells of death that nearly choked him if he had to remove those splatters and body parts when he scoured the cabs before he tinkered with the engines.

But other visions popped into his dreams, some of them even more unsettling than the gruesome interiors of the choppers. Shortly after Mick had arrived in Alaska, he started hanging out on weekends with other inductees, mainly privates, like himself, and some corporals. One of the guys in their group Richard, an eighteen-year-old kid with olive skin, deep-set brown eyes, a slender build, and black, curly hair, was friendly and comical, and everyone liked him. Unfortunately, when Richard got too wasted, he'd often head back to the barracks, dig into his trunk, and pull out women's panties, bras, and flimsy dresses to become a cross-dresser. Although the rest of the guys in the squad accepted this, much like members in the 407 M*A*S*H* unit accepted Corporal Klinger's antics, they didn't encourage his returning to the town as a woman later.

And unlike Klinger, Richard didn't cross-dress to get kicked out of the army. In fact, he'd enlisted. He cross-dressed because he wanted to become a woman, at least, when he was plastered. And it seemed to Mick with the sort of wardrobe Richard selected, he must have wanted to be a female whore. He'd like to slip into the frilliest underclothes and slinky, glittery dresses, wrap himself in either a red or yellow boa, and wear long, dangling earrings. Then, he'd pull on a wig, smear on blue eye shadow and black eyeliner, and rub maroon red over his lips. Plus, he'd wear the highest spike heels he could find in a size thirteen. Mick and the other soldiers admitted that Richard made a fairly attractive, even sexy, girl.

This went on for several months. Every two weeks or so, after the squad went out to the bars in Barrow, the men would go back to their quarters and Richard would dig into his trunk and play dress-up. What none of the men had realized, though, was that sometimes Richard slipped out for long walks during the wee hours when he was dressed in drag.

Then, late one night after an evening of partying at one of the bars in Barrow, Mick sauntered back to his bunk and there was Richard, in full feminine regalia, sprawled across it. It seemed he'd even applied false eyelashes—they were long and fluttery, looking almost like spider legs, Mick thought. Richard had crossed one leg over the other, and leaning one of his cheeks on a wrist, his elbow on the bed, he spoke in breathy tones. "Won't you drive me into town, Big Boy?" He fluttered his spidery lashes. "There's a guy I'm supposed to meet there."

"What?" This was a bit too much for Mick to swallow. "A guy? Where?"

"Not just any guy, silly." Richard spoke now in a falsetto. "He's a big, tough marine. He was patrolling the area one night when I took a walk. We made a date to meet at The Gold Pan."

The Gold Pan was a bar in town mainly frequented by locals. Mick and his buddies generally went to another tavern, Mike's, down the street from The Pan.

Mick shook his head and stared at Richard a long time. "I dunno. Does this guy know who you are—I mean underneath it all."

Richard shrugged. "He likes me, I can tell." He fluttered his eyelashes again and leaned back and pulled fingers through his hair. "The night we met, he gave me a ride back to base. And well, I gave him one sweet goodnight kiss with a sweet caress across his crotch." With that, he fluttered the fingers on one of his hands. The nails were long and red.

"Spare me the details, buddy." Plopping onto the corner of the bunk, Mick lowered his head.

"And how did you grow your fingernails so long— they'd never pass inspection."

Richard smiled and drew in his chin. "They're falsies, silly. Just like some other appendages on me."

Today, even when Mick wasn't dreaming, he'd still picture Richard posing on his bunk, especially after a long night of boozing. And along with the scene of Richard, these images—the maroon lipstick, the long, red fingernails, the blue eye shadow and spike heels— kept recurring in Mick's dreams. Sometimes, he found them so alluring, he'd request Judith to don such polish, shadow, and heels. When they were first married, she did. But after she'd seen a photograph of her and Mick, together, she quit wearing them. These items weren't her style, she said. "The colors make me look like either a whore—or a clown."

Mick often considered that what happened later that night might have caused visions of Richard to continually pop up in his mind. After whining and begging, Richard had finally convinced Mick to drive him to The Gold Pan, where Mick left him on a barstool, looking like a typical barfly. Richard didn't show up in base all night or the next day, either. So the sergeant sent out his squad to find him. The men drove through the town, then searched all the surrounding area, the plains of snow and thick groves of pine. They were about to embark on a trek up one of the mountains when they spotted a red Ford pickup that appeared to be stuck in a snow drift.

Ben, the private driving the jeep honked, but no one in the truck responded. Yet, it appeared that a person sat on the passenger's side in the cab. When they neared the Ford, they identified Richard, still in his feminine attire, leaning against a window. He appeared to be passed-out because he didn't flinch when Ben honked again. "What's going on?" he said. "Wonder where Rich got that truck."

Mick said nothing at first, then he volunteered, "Pull up about twenty feet from it, not too close. I'll check it out." He whipped out his pistol and approached the Ford.

What he saw then seared his brains, leaving them with a black brand that he knew he'd never undo. The images from that night would stay inside him forever. First, he'd looked around to see if the marine Richard had mentioned were lurking somewhere. Seeing no one around, he knocked on the window near Richard. He still didn't move. Mick tried the handle. The door was unlocked so he opened it. First, he saw that Richard's wig was pulled to one side and someone had torn the bodice of his dress. His boa was twisted into a knot and jammed between his legs. Then Mick spotted the blood running from just under Richard's Adam's apple, down his neck, and into the dress, drenched with it. Keeping his glove on, Mick gently lifted Richard's head. His neck had been slit, clean across. Quickly, Mick withdrew his hand. "God!" he said and waved the others to join him.

Mick never forgave himself for allowing Richard to talk him into a ride to The Gold Pan. His gut had told him not to do it, but he couldn't convince Richard otherwise. In fact, he only gave in when Richard had threatened to ask someone else. Even so, later, Mick wished he would've knocked the kid out. He might have been bruised, but maybe he would've lived.

So Richard would often come into Mick's dreams, mixed with images of his attire, but also mixed with battle scenes and helicopters filled with blood and guts. One more image kept recurring, too. Even if it wasn't bloody or gruesome, the image remained an eerie one, an image that no matter how much he drank, he couldn't shake from his brains, an image that too many times, made him tremble.

One night during his Alaska tour, the army received some sort of alert. Mick never learned the details about who sent it, and he never understood any of the underpinnings of what he saw that night, either. Nonetheless, the officers ordered Mick's platoon to meet in full uniform as they did for reveille, except for this alert—or drill—Mick to this day was unsure which, they met at one a.m.

It was during the Alaskan winter, too, when the skies never clearly showed the sun. Instead, each day contained only about an hour of thin light, more like twilight really. So the night was eerie, with black clouds forming across the purple skies, and the air so crisp and still that Mick felt almost as if they were on another planet. Being a Midwestern boy, used to thick trees, sweaty, humid summers, and fairly long hours on sunlight, even in the winters, he never truly adapted to the Alaska climate. Of course, the booze helped, as it always had helped him to adapt, and sometimes, cocaine worked to keep him alert. But when he was outside on nights such as that one, it seemed at the time he experienced it, that the entire environment was a strange, surreal dream.

The men had been in formation for a few minutes, awaiting orders to do who knew what—everyone, even the sergeants, seemed as confused as the privates—when suddenly, out of a mountain just north of the base, an intense light containing streaks of red, gold, and a silvery white, emanated from one of the mountains and rose like lasers high into the black sky. Mick had witnessed the northern lights, but this was something different, especially because somehow, a slit in the mountain opened to let out the light. And the slit was between something metallic, as if convex steel shields had opened. It looked like something from *Star Wars*.

Apparently, the military had built something within that mountain. But none of the men had known anything about it. No one had briefed them about this. They hadn't even heard rumors about any operation going on in that mountain. The situation was eerie, yes, but Mick always played the good soldier, He'd follow orders to the T and his uniform and shoes remained impeccable. He'd learned that from his father, who'd made him and his brother spit and buff their shoes every morning. In fact, they had to get out of bed a half an hour early to do so. So he was used to taking orders without questioning them, just as he did the night the mountain opened. But the image of the mountain and the light emanating from it kept appearing in his dreams again lately, and he couldn't figure out why.

Chapter Twenty-One
Krystal's Hopes Delayed

Mick's just lucky that Momma and I love cats. If it weren't for Christine, he woulda had to stay in the crummy apartment he got downtown after Momma told him to leave.

About six months ago, Mamma's cat Cali, who was older than me, finally died. Her kidneys failed. About three days before she went, her face bloated and she quit eating and drinking. It was me that found her curled into a furry ball on the couch. Because she often slept that way and Momma was busy sticking her nose into law books, she didn't pay much attention to the cat. She patted Cali and headed up to her room to study.

I spotted Cali, and because it was a Friday night, I figured I'd have time to play with her. So I tickled the back of her neck to rouse her. But she ignored me. Then, when I lifted her up, I saw her face had swelled till she looked like a furry marshmallow. I took her up to Momma's room and put her on the bed. "Look at your cat!" I snapped.

Momma, of course, went berserk. She frantically called her brother, who was a doctor and asked him what could be wrong with Cali. He diagnosed her with kidney failure. At least, Momma wasn't so crazy as to try to put the cat on dialysis. On the other hand, I wondered if she woulda done it if it weren't so expensive. She'd had that cat all her adult life, seventeen years, she said, and I believed her. So the cat was about only eighteen years old, which Momma said is still too young for a housecat to die.

She just pleaded with Cali, tried to get her to eat something, or at least, drink some water. She even shoved milk out for her, which she didn't often let her drink. Cali couldn't walk right anymore, either. She'd scoot across the kitchen linoleum and drag her back legs. On Sunday, she finally drank a tiny bit of water and Momma shouted with joy. I mean, you could hear her all over the house.

Well, that cat hung in there Sunday, and Momma had set her up in a basket with bedding and blankets. She'd bought the basket for Cali the year before, but the cat wouldn't stay in it very long—until her last couple of days when she was so sick. Momma was so worried about her, she slept on the couch by the basket so she could scratch Cali under her chin and in between her ears, the places that she liked to be petted and scratched the most.

The next day was Martin Luther King Day, and that was good, because we were out of school and Mick was off work because it was a Monday. After staying beside the cat overnight and the next morning—she even did her exercises in the living room so she could keep an eye on Cali—Momma had to run to the store for milk or some other emergency. When she got home, she decided to call the vet to find out whether it was Tylenol or an aspirin that you could give a cat for pain without hurting it. (Now, I thought at this point it wouldn't matter since Cali was dying, but Momma gets strangely illogical during those emotional times.) She also thought he might have another pain reliever she could use. She'd decided that Cali would be happier staying with us than going to some stinking vet, who'd put her down. But she didn't want the cat to suffer, either.

Then, the saddest thing happened. The vet's number was busy, and when Momma held the receiver to her ear and simultaneously checked on Cali, she noticed the blanket covering the cat no longer swelled and collapsed. Cali was gone.

Momma cried and cried. I wondered if she'd cry that much if something happened to me or Adam. Mick and Adam went outside and dug a hole, then we put Cali, still wrapped in her blanket, into a cardboard box that we set in the chair in the kitchen so we could have a funeral.

Because of the holiday, my dad was in town that weekend. So Momma even asked him to the funeral, being that they were still together when she got Cali. In fact, my dad had picked her out at the pound when my mother was at work. She thought it was only right that he be there, too. So Adam, Mick, my dad, Momma, and I all sat around Cali's cardboard casket and talked about what each of us would especially miss about her. Then Momma sang a hymn. It's good that our service didn't go on any longer, either, because some fleas started crawling out of Cali's fur. It made Momma so mad that she got the Black Flag and just smothered them till Cali's face looked foamy, too. Along with being so swollen, the foam made her look like she had died from either from some sort of rabies or she'd fallen into a washing machine during the sudsy cycle.

Adam and Mick buried Cali out back under the tree where Zebyn had given all of us such a scare. Except for the time when Zebyn possessed that tree, Cali had liked to wander around there, and she'd often rubbed against its bark. So we thought it was an appropriate burial ground. Then, Momma wore all black for the next three weeks everywhere she went, including to law school. Most of the students were compassionate, especially when Momma shared the part about scratching Cali's head the night before. But Tanner said something stupid then that showed sometimes he could be an idiot, almost as bad as Mick. In fact, Kerri, the cutest law student, the one I had my eye on, snapped at Tanner for being so "insensitive."

After that cat died, Momma became awfully quiet for long stretches of time. And then, one evening she picked me up from school and dropped me off at home because she was going to meet with other students to cram for a midterm. She hadn't wanted to leave me with Mick, but she'd made him promise he wouldn't drink while he was looking after me. Well, that jerk started popping open Budweisers before the dust cleared from the driveway after Momma left. I went to my room so I wouldn't have to listen to him blabber. When Momma returned two hours later, he lay in a drunken stupor on the sofa.

Momma said nothing, but the next morning, she told him to get out. I was glad, too. But after awhile,

I missed him a little, even if he was a creep. It was odd, what I missed most was his mediocrity. See, Momma and Adam were so creative, I figured I was just no match for them. But Mick, even if he could build some interesting furniture, just wasn't the creative type. So when he was around, I felt better about my lack of talent. This was especially important now that Cindy and Sherry had moved away. They were mainly into clothes, toys, and boys—not artwork, reading novels, or performing music. So I felt smart around them, except when Cindy tried to bully me. Anyway, after Mick left, I especially missed Cindy and Sherry, too.

A couple of days after Momma kicked him out, Mick got an apartment and moved most of his stuff in it. For the next two days, we didn't hear from him. Then Mick phoned Momma every day.

"Oh, come see my apartment," he'd say. "You'll like it," as if Momma should move in with him or something. Then, he came by every weekend when he was off work. She'd cry every time he left, too, even though she was just sick that he wouldn't quit drinking.

This went on for about two months. Then, one Saturday night when Mick wasn't there, I spotted a cat on television that one of the newscasters, Laurie Everett, was trying to get people to adopt. "Momma, come here!" I yelled. "This cat's called a tortoise shell."

Momma saw it and I could tell she fell in love. Her eyes were brighter than they'd been when Joe played his guitar in the back yard gig. "She's beautiful." Momma sighed and plopped into a chair. "Plus, she's already spayed and her front claws de-clawed," she said excitedly.

But then she frowned. "Too bad we can't get her."

"Why not?" I said. "You said she's beautiful. And I can help take care of her."

"Because of the money." She sighed and still looking at the cat on TV, plopped onto the couch. "Or lack thereof. Even if we stretch the budget to pay for the adoption fee and the license, we'll have to buy food and litter for her. And for any more cats I own, I'm not buying cheap cat food. I think that's what killed Cali. No more!"

It made me sad to suggest it, but I could see no other way. I knew Momma needed another cat back in her life to help her get over Cali, and I figured somehow we could keep Mick in line, and I have to admit, I felt a little bit sorry for Mick, him living in such a lousy neighborhood and all, so I said it. "What if Mick moves back in? Then could we afford the cat?"

Momma stared at me. "Are you sure you'll be okay with that? The choice is yours. You're the one who was damaged the most here. What if you'd fallen or something? I mean, I'll never leave you alone with him again, even if he does stop drinking. I can never take that chance again, ever."

The night before, after Grandma had given us free tickets, Momma and I saw "Phantom" at Starlight Theater, so when we spotted the cat in the back of the shelter, we called her "Christine" after the heroine in the musical. Amazingly, she answered when we called, and that's been her name ever since.

So Mick moved back into our house. Adam still lived in the basement, which helped, too. At first, Adam was angry we let Mick return after what happened. But Adam also knew this would allow Momma to finish law school. Otherwise, she'd have to drop-out, and she'd never make enough money to support us on her own.

A few months later, she tried taking Mick on a trip to Vegas with hopes of mending their mess of a marriage, but that didn't work, either. He started drinking on the plane, she explained later, and he didn't let up for the entire trip, which made it one more bummer for Momma. Then Adam moved out, which was a bummer for me.

Chapter Twenty-Two
Adam Freaks

Even though Adam liked his mother's neighborhood, he liked being away from civilization in the country with Allie, too. And Allie particularly liked having him around to help her build fences and fix her plumbing. She enjoyed sleeping with him, too, or so she'd told him, many times.

"You're the best I've ever had," she'd claimed. This especially made Adam feel good when he later discovered that during high school, Allie had dated one of Adam's older cousins, Don. Don had always bragged about his expertise in the bedroom. Don had dated at least four times as many women as Adam had, and he'd slept with at least ten times more. And now, one of Don's ex-girlfriends considered Adam superior. His ego needed this boost.

So despite forebodings about the possibility of clashes between their strong personalities, Adam spent more and more time at Allie's. He gradually transferred more and more of his belongings into her trailer, until he'd more or less moved in completely.

Unfortunately, his classes suffered. In fact, he had to withdraw from all of them except the writing class and music theory class. At least, he was still earning A's in them.

Other than that, living with Allie had been good for him. He'd started working outside, hammering together fences from planks, even stringing barbed wire across the top, which helped build his strength. He liked the smells around the farm, too, especially the smell of wet wood after a rain. It felt good to fill his lungs with the fresh air unpolluted with car exhaust, smog, and smoke from chimneys. Yes, the workouts and fresh air were good for his lungs, even if he continued smoking.

And recently, Allie told Adam he could add on a studio to her trailer, so he'd been working on that. For a long time, he'd wanted a studio to record in, and now, it appeared that dream was on the brink of happening. He liked Allie, too, even if he wasn't sure he loved her. Their sex was good: It was tender, but at the same time, lively and fun. He especially liked the way she kissed him so passionately. Allie helped him build his survival instinct, too. She showed him where the county healthcare offices were located so he could receive medical care and prescriptions for pennies, if he had to pay anything at all for him. He thought it was ironic that Allie knew how to obtain benefits when her parents had so much money. Of course, she was over eighteen, so they no longer had to provide any doctors or medications for her.

On the other hand, she wasn't very domestic. In fact, she spent little time preparing food or cleaning house. These weren't Adam's priorities, either. So they ate frequently at fast-food restaurants, especially Sonic, McDonald's, and Denny's, and they stepped over socks, jeans, candy and cigarette wrappers and bits of papers cluttering their carpets. Consequently, life with Allie was both good and bad for Adam. Although occasionally, they socialized at a couple of coffee shops near the university in Kansas City, they spent most evenings jamming, Allie on the flute and Adam on the keyboards after they'd smoked a bong or two. So somehow music had soothed their strong personalities, and generally Allie and Adam lived in harmony.

The dog's attitude toward Adam, however, remained a problem. Bruiser liked him no more after the two months Adam had lived there than the dog had the first time the two creatures met. Bruiser would growl at him even when Adam fed him, and sometimes, the dog snapped at him.

After one morning, when Allie had taken her car into town, and the dog had acted more persnickety than usual, growling then nipping Adam's fingers when he dropped dog food into his bowl, Adam could take it no more. He blew up. Losing all restraints, he slammed the dog's bowl against the wall. "Damn, you!" yelled and stamped a foot. "Lay off or get out of here! Get!"

Instead of backing down, Bruiser grew angry, even angrier than Adam. The dog turned around, growled again, snapped, and leapt toward Adam. Even though Adam tried to duck, the beast moved too fast. He landed on his chest and knocked him to the floor. He growled louder now and bared his teeth. Adam saw the black edging the animal's huge incisors and suddenly, he reacted.

Moving on instinct without scheming a plan, he grabbed the dog's jaw and held it, then he wrapped himself around the beast, causing the two of them to roll over and over, becoming a strange wheel of fur, sweat pants, and flesh. Trying to shimmy out of Adam's clutch, the dog wiggled and thrashed but the animal couldn't break loose. Still, he kicked at Adam and swiped him, his claws drawing blood, which jumpstarted Adam's adrenaline. He grabbed the dog by the back of the neck, then pressed a knee against one of his shoulders and pinned the animal to the floor. With strength that seemed to come from some supernatural source, he held the dog's mouth shut and sat on top of him. Despite the dog's writhing, Adam managed to press his other hand firmly against Bruiser's jugular. Like some madman caught up in the frenzy of a battle of wills for some territory or high ideals, Adam pressed harder and harder. The beast wiggled his head and legs and tried o thrash, but he kept his hands firmly on the dog's neck. Then Adam jerked the dog's head and hit it again and again against the linoleum until he heard something snap. The animal went limp but still tried to lift and turn its head a couple of times until finally, whining in a strange, fluttering tone, almost like a whinny, he let out a low moan and in a few seconds, no longer took in another breath.

His heart pounding, Adam withdrew his hand and shook it. He felt tears rim his eyes when looked at Bruiser's corpse. He looked at it a long, long time. He hadn't meant to kill the thing. But the animal's teeth had scared him. And then, he'd become caught up in the battle. Events like this made him worry that something might be wrong with his brain. Why had he gone nuts when the dog attacked? Wasn't there a more civilized way to handle it? Then again, there was no way he could have walked outside to cool off once Bruiser lunged at him. He envisioned the scene again and again. But no matter how many times he replayed it, it still seemed surreal, as if he'd stumbled into some movie or video game that he hadn't intended to play.

He worried even more about Allie's reaction. He wasn't sure how he'd explain this to her. Even if she'd already considered taking the dog to the vet to be put down, he still feared how she'd respond to the news, and he didn't feel optimistic about the outcome. At least, the battle hadn't left much blood, and what was there had belonged to him. Nevertheless, he was concerned about what to do with the body. Obviously, he couldn't leave it in the kitchen, but he didn't think he could bury it outside, either. A front from the west had plummeted temperatures so low, the last few nights they'd suffered a hard freeze. So he wasn't sure that even if he pushed on it with all his weight, the garden hoe could break through the icy ground.

He glanced at the dog once more then walked to

the kitchen window and looked at the land in the back yard edging the pasture. It looked icy, rock hard. Suddenly, he spotted the shed, which gave him an idea. With it being so cold, he could slide the dog into a large plastic bag, put it into the shed, where it'd freeze. Then, when it became warm enough to dig a hole for the body, he'd dig Bruiser a proper grave.

By the time he'd rifled through the cabinets and found a box of Hefty bags, pulled one out and opened it, then tried to side it under the dog, *rigor mortis* had started to make bending the limbs difficult. Plus, the dog had died with his legs splayed, so Adam couldn't fit him into plastic shroud. Still clutching the bag, he sat cross-legged on the linoleum and tried to figure out how to inch the dog into it. He had no choice, he decided, but to saw off the animal's legs.

Having read some old navy books about surgery at his grandparents' house, he understood that he sawing through the joints would work faster than trying to saw across the femurs. If he could bend the front joints backwards, too, he'd have less area to saw, and he'd only have to operate on two legs. Perhaps one, if he were especially lucky, he might be able to maneuver the stiffening legs of the beast into a shape that would slide into the bag.

He wasn't sure when Allie would arrive, either, and he wanted the mess to be in the shed, all the fur and any blood wiped away, before she walked into the kitchen. Even if he'd still have to explain what happened, the shock would be less if he prepared her before she saw her dog in this sad state. He wondered if there were some way he could close the dog's eyes. Their dull stare had started to bother him.

He dug into the tool box shoved in a corner in the cabinet under the kitchen sink. He pulled out two saws—one with wide teeth, the other, a hack saw—and wondered which one would work best. He'd seen antique surgeon's saws that looked more like the standard version, but he instinctively chose the hack saw, perhaps because it was lighter. "Follow your gut" had become his motto when he worked on household repairs or other projects for which he hadn't previously outlined a plan of attack, and today, especially, with the way things had been going, he figured he'd better stay with his regular M.O.

He'd just pulled the hack saw out of the box and had started to decide the exact place to pierce the skin when suddenly, he smelled something burning. He glanced at the stove. No red lights shone, so neither the oven nor the burners were on. Still clutching the hammer, he arose and wandered through the trailer. Not even an electric blanket was turned on. He thought the smell might have been dust burning in the heating vents, but the fan hadn't gone on for a while. After poking his head into each of the three tiny bedrooms, he threw on his jacket and stepped outside.

The air was as chilly as it looked from inside the house, and gray clouds had started to roil into masses that would likely bring snow. It smelled like snow to him, and he hoped it wouldn't fall so heavily they'd have trouble driving on their nearly bald tires. He scanned the fields, searching for smoke or a flame that created the smell. He saw nothing nearby, but he saw something flicker on the distant horizon. He wasn't sure if it was an unattended brush fire, or if someone burned leaves or old grass. He squinted in the direction for a few seconds then decided to return to the mess he had to clean up before Allie arrived. He glanced at his watch. Already, it was eleven-thirty, and he didn't know what time she'd left. He pulled a pack of cigarettes from his coat pocket and started to take out one. Then it dawned on him that he might have left one burning.

Scrambling back to the house, he dashed inside and ran to the bathroom sink, where, on a ledge encircling the sink, a cigarette balanced. It had burned out, leaving a long, perfectly formed cylinder of ash. Quickly, he wet a few squares of toilet paper, wrapped the butt in it, and tossed it into the kitchen trash, where he hoped Allie wouldn't see it. At least, he reassured himself, he'd had some good luck today, and he reminded himself never to light a cigarette when no ashtray was around. Then he returned to the floor and began pulling the saw through one of the joints at the top of one of Bruiser's front legs.

Sawing it wasn't easy, and soon he realized he'd have to shove paper towels underneath the section where he carved to ensure he wouldn't leave a mess. So he had to stop to find the towels. He sawed again and finally, after stopping and twisting the dog's joint, he was able to break the leg away from the body. He threw it into the bag and tried to position the dog inside it, too. It wouldn't quite fit. He'd have to lop off the other leg, he was sure now. He glanced at the clock. It was a little after twelve noon.

Cutting the other leg went a little faster, but not much. And it seemed the tendons and sinews on that joint held tighter than those had on the other one. Still he worked on, glancing every few minutes at the clock, and intermittently looking out the picture window where he'd see Allie's Saab arrive. He worked wildly now. In fact, he sawed so hard, he sweated and he felt heat spread from the back of his neck to his shoulders. But he couldn't stop now. Once the other leg came off, he was sure the dog would find in the bag and he could drag the entire mess to the shed.

Amazingly, he finished amputating the other leg, and he was able to fit the corpse into the bag. After he crammed it into the shed, he returned and cleaned up the kitchen. He started to throw away the dog's bowls, too, but he retrieved them from the trash. Perhaps he'd buy Allie another pet, a gentle dog that liked him. He rinsed out the dishes and slid them under the sink.

After he finished, he pulled out his keyboard and started forming an odd melody, one with diminished chords and high Fs. If he didn't accomplish much else today, besides, of course, killing a dog, maybe he could write a sonata or something short. He wondered if he should work on something with lighter chords.

Allie came home cheerful and chattered about her grocery shopping expedition. She shoved grapes and bing cherries into the refrigerator and boxes of crackers into the cabinet. So she'd been home at least twenty minutes when she noticed Bruiser's absence.

"I'm sorry," Adam said. "But the dog had gone wild. He attacked me." Tears rimmed his eyes again but didn't roll down his cheeks. "I didn't mean to kill him, but we were spinning and he kept growling, and well, I got angry and scared at the same time. I was afraid because Bruiser attacked me, and I guess I went berserk."

"Really?" Allie raised her eyebrows. Then she turned away from Adam and with her head bowed, moved slowly toward the bedroom. She said nothing else but went inside the room and closed the door. She didn't come out for a long, long time.

Chapter Twenty-Three
Judith Bites Her Tongue

"But the dog was trying to kill you, right?" Judith raised her voice as she talked into the receiver. "It was self-defense. What else could you do?"

Adam's voice, on the other hand, had lowered to a drone. "That isn't what upset her so much. It was mainly because I chopped up the dog."

"What? You didn't eat him, did you?" Judith worried that perhaps Adam's interest in Asian cultures had gone too far. She could hear Adam chuckle a little at her response, even though until then he'd sounded depressed.

"No, I didn't actually chop him up—just had to

cut off his legs to fit him into the plastic bag. Allie thinks I'm crazy for touching a corpse."

"She knew the name of your band." Judith hesitated, hoping that Adam would see the humor, the irony. "That should've forewarned her."

"You're probably right," he responded, but he didn't sound very cheerful.

At least, by being alone all day, Judith had finished studying and grading. Krystal had stayed with her father that weekend, and Mick had to cover some employee's late shift, or so he said. So she was free to drive all the way to Cleveland, Missouri, and beyond to pick up Adam. Although she was happy to have Adam return home, where she felt he was safer, she hated to see him in pain. The tone of his voice signaled her that Allie meant quite a bit to him. So far, Allie hadn't impressed anyone else in the household. Krystal and she didn't like her stand-offish attitude and had dubbed her "Allie-Fonté," but of course, they never used the endearing name in front of Adam. And Mick had seemed completely oblivious to the girl.

Actually, Judith hadn't disliked Allie but she worried about her influence upon Adam. In fact, even though Adam's withdrawal from college had dismayed Judith, she hoped he'd find some happiness with Allie. So that Saturday evening when he phoned her, his words "Come get me" sank her into an awful sadness. She worried that her dysfunctional relationships with husbands had impacted Adam so much he might not be able to function in a relationship. But what could she do about the past? She had only tried to survive, too, in what appeared to be impossible situations.

It was after six and already dark in February. Still, the sky looked clear, and the air had a chill, but it wasn't too cold. That was a blessing. Still, Judith wished Mick had been home, so he would do the treacherous drive. Even though it didn't look or feel as if any clouds would blow in rain or snow to create scary road conditions, Judith worried about getting lost. She'd never been to Cleveland. Adam had said it was south—rather far south—around 150th and Holmes, and he detailed the directions from Holmes Road to the farm.

But Judith hadn't been that far south on Holmes. She'd never been south of 131st street, also Blue Ridge Boulevard, a street near her mother's house. She knew 135th Street became Highway 150, which ran west into Olathe. But she wasn't sure what landmarks would point out 150th Street and how she'd see it in the dark.

She sighed. She hoped if she continued driving south on Holmes Road, she'd surely find the place. Oh, she hated driving at night when she couldn't easily read street signs and pick out other landmarks. Nevertheless, Judith would journey after her son, bring him back home to warmth and safety. She'd worried, anyway, whether he'd been eating properly and receiving medical care in his new country home. And she wondered if the young couple took precautions against pregnancy—and STDs. So her feelings about the situation were mixed. Mainly, she worried about how to help Adam's self esteem. Perhaps it was time for her and Krystal to use the name "Allie-Fonté" in Adam's presence.

Only about a mile and a half-east, Holmes Road wasn't far from where she lived. So she turned on it in a few minutes and drove due south beyond many sights she'd seen on her long treks to Longview Community College. Plus, at 99th and Holmes, a restaurant and bar still stood where Joe had performed regular gigs for about two years. Those had been better times during their relationship, so passing the place usually made her smile. For a second, she pictured him strumming his guitar, playing his masterpiece, "Picadilly Circus," named after the square in London.

Few rock or folk lyrics contained such detailed, sensual descriptions, and even fewer songs blended the lyrics with the rhythms, rifts, and guitar licks that echoed and reverberated to send her wading through warm seawater, a soothing liquid at the temperature that melted the waves into her skin. To tell the truth, many times, Judith wondered if she missed that song more than she did him. Although she owned a tape of it with their other originals, the tape didn't sound nearly as good as the group did live. In fact, the tape made them sound as if they'd recorded the cuts from the opposite end of an underground tunnel from a mike.

Plus, today, certainly, it'd be more convenient if she had a CD, but there was no way to get one. Unfortunately, with his group being unknown nationally, no one would ever cover that song, and it was unlikely he and his partner would record it again or burn it onto a CD. She didn't know if Streetside Records in Westport still sold their tapes, and she no longer found time to check out the store.

Tonight, thinking about Joe and his music made her chuckle. It was ironic—Joe had once chided her for attending his gigs only to see him—not to hear him perform. And now, she knew that his music mattered more to her than he had. It's why she'd hung around him for so long. Joe had a crappy personality: Always flashing hot and cold, he was either overly amorous or accusing her of "hidden agendas," agendas which she didn't have at all. Sometimes his accusations had caused her to question if maybe she'd held such "agendas" in her subconscious. At least, now that she hadn't seen him in years, she realized, no, she hadn't. She missed the music—the music drew her to him. He'd been only the transmitter—a Kokopelli really—of something much grander than any human being. She'd hoped to be the same sort of medium with her writing.

She drove past the shopping center with the bar, past Red Bridge Road, also known as 111th Street, past 131th Street, also known as Blue Ridge Boulevard, and finally, she passed 135th Street or 151 Highway. That was it—all her known territory. She ventured into the wild now. She wished she would've remembered her cell phone, but she'd gone too far to go back for it. She turned up the radio. Hoping soft music would calm her, she tuned in a Christian station.

A talk show aired, and a broadcaster interviewed Miller Fuller, the man who'd founded Habitat for Humanity in 1976. Judith had believed that Jimmy Carter started the charity. But she'd been mistaken. Instead, no politician, no government leader had done so. Instead, the charity had been founded by a private individual who'd once been a lawyer. Then recently, after thirty years, the organization kicked Fuller out of it. "On January 3, I turned seventy," he recalled. "And on January 31, I was without a job." Yet, unlike the author Bettie Younger, who written the book *The House that Love Built* about Fuller and his wife and their mission, Fuller never resented the organization for "stealing" Habitat for Humanity. "It wasn't stolen from me," he explained. "I never owned it. God owned it."

Miller had been led to found the charity, he said, when his wife almost divorced him because he'd been a workaholic. He claimed he'd enveloped her in a mansion with surrounding acreage, lakes, pools, and stables, but added, "She didn't have a husband. I was always working."

Judith turned up the radio louder. She wondered if along with being an alcoholic, Mick weren't a workaholic, too. Unfortunately, instead of dumping all the funds he earned from his hard work into an estate, he was putting the liquor store owner's children through college. She wished so much that she could get through to Mick—that her mixed-up husband could come to a realization similar to Miller Fuller's.

But Fuller ran on faith more than Judith did.

Surprisingly, when he gave up his career to win back his wife, the two of them gave up their estate. They committed themselves to do whatever God wanted them to do and go wherever he wanted them to go. Somehow He gave them the word, and they started Habitat for Humanity. They also became missionaries to such places as the Congo.

Tonight, on the radio, Fuller also claimed "the Lord is faithful." After leaving Habitat, he'd formed the Fuller Center for Housing, which recently committed to build sixty homes for hurricane victims in Shreveport, Louisiana. "We've built forty of them already," he said. "And a hundred houses in El Salvador, many in the Congo, and in Bloomington, Illinois." Many employees from Habitat joined the organization, which was going as strong as the Habitat did in its beginning years.

Judith thought it odd, though, that she hadn't heard of the Fuller Center. During the past two years, the media gave the *Extreme Makeover* crew all the attention. Nevertheless, this guy Fuller appeared awfully chipper, and twice now, he lost everything then gained everything. *So either he was right about the Lord, or he was just terribly lucky,* Judith decided.

She looked ahead at the two-lane road with its crisp white and yellow lines, imitating a county highway. Hers was the only vehicle going either direction. By now, a gibbous moon hit against the hundreds of deciduous trees—oaks and maples—and caused long shadows to splash across the asphalt. The highway stretched forever south, and with the black shadows over the pavement, the scene became surreal for Judith. She looked at the next sign marking the cross street. It was 145th, so she must be nearing the farm, she figured.

But she found no street sign at what she'd estimated to be 150th Street, and then, she began to worry. Still, scanning the sides of the road for a gas station where she could ask directions, she kept driving south. She hoped she hadn't passed the turn, but she hadn't seen a sign beyond 147th Street.

Finally, after driving what seemed to be forever, but was likely only three minutes more, Judith pulled into a gas station. At first, she worried because the parking lot lights had been dimmed. The lights on the building and on the large neon-framed sign weren't that bright, either. She worried that the station might be closed. Or perhaps the place was being robbed, and the robber demanded that the clerk turn down the lights. She glanced around. It was the only building within the vicinity sporting any lights at all. Other than the moon and the occasional street lights, the surrounding area was a deep purple mixed with black. Then, she saw a flash of movement inside the building. She spotted a clerk behind the counter, so she went inside and asked how far she was from Cleveland.

"Cleveland?" The clerk, a red-haired kid who looked eighteen and couldn't be more than 21, chuckled. "You're going the right direction, but it's a lot further south."

"How much farther?" Judith began to feel nervous and twitched her nose . In fact, I thought it was around 150th Street. I thought I passed it."

He chuckled again. "You have a long way yet to

go." He grinned. "You need more like 250th Street."

Judith frowned. "I hope the street's marked there."

"Don't worry. There's a highway sign marking Cleveland city limits. You can't miss it."

At least, Judith felt a bit more confident about traveling onwards, but the miles and miles farther south began to irritate her. She wished Adam would have been more precise about the location and worried that his detailed directions to the trailer might not be accurate, either. He'd warned her that the last part of the trail would be a muddy, gravel road, so she wore boots to be prepared for the area around the place he called "the farm," especially with the ground being so wet from the rains earlier in the week.

She drove on and on, and when she veered off of Holmes and followed Adam's directions, the landmarks he'd mentioned were all where they should have been.

But Adam had neglected to prepare her for the sloppy conditions under which he'd been living with Allie. Although her first impulse was to blame her son, who hadn't kept anywhere near a meticulous bed room when he'd lived with her. But she knew Adam was not responsible for the bathroom wastebasket overflowing with used tampons spilling onto the floor. Even though sometimes Judith's home became cluttered with portfolios, books, and other papers, this sort of slovenliness she couldn't abide. She was amazed that Adam hadn't complained about the conditions. Plus, piles of clothes, some with smelly underarms, others with slashes of mud around the edge of the legs, lie in heaps on the floor in both the bathroom and the bedroom. Judith wiped the toilet carefully and spread tissues over the seat as she would at a public restroom. After she finished, she called to Adam. "Don't you guys ever do washing?"

"We've got to do them at the laundromat. And there isn't one close by."

Judith knew he wasn't lying about that. She helped him stuff his dirty clothes into large, black plastic bags, probably from the same box that provided one for Bruiser's shroud, and they loaded what little furniture he had into the Saturn, which remarkably, held more than she'd anticipated. Fortunately, the back seats could fold flat.

"You'll have to have Mick drive you down here Monday and help you get those two tables. They won't fit." Glad she'd emptied everything from the trunk but the jumper cables before she'd left the house, she stuffed everything as far back as she could, and listened for the click when closed the trunk door. "Whew! I was afraid we couldn't take very much with us tonight. Certainly, not this much."

Since she'd stepped inside the trailer, Adam's mood had remained somber. But now, he softly chuckled.

Chapter Twenty-Four
Krystal Bides

Boy—was I glad to have Adam back home and away from smelly Allie-Fonté! Try as I might, I just couldn't force myself to like her, and I don't think Momma did much either. Allie always raised her nose in the air when she talked to me, as if I was some sort of crud on someone's pants leg. Adam seemed to be okay about being with us again, except he was always so sad. He kept blaming himself for "losing Allie," and on Valentine's Day, he went out and bought her a bouquet of red roses, which he took to her at Muddy's, where she started working part-time right after he left. He said she looked at him funny when he gave them to her. Me, I thought he'd wasted his money. I would've bought some Valentine's Day candy for the entire family, or at least, for my mom and sister.

At first, he slept on Momma's antique couch from the 1920s, until she bought him an army cot to set up in her office. Then, after he'd been living with us about three weeks, he said he was going to commit himself to an institution. Because he was nineteen by then, he said Momma wouldn't have to pay for it. In fact, he wouldn't have to either because he made so little money working part-time at The Haven. So Momma took him downtown to Western State, which had to admit him because he said he felt suicidal. Later, he told me that he'd rattled on and on about killing Allie's dog, just to let them know that he was a "danger to himself and others."

The problem was, he shared a room with other guys who were far more dangerous. He told me about one of his roommates on the phone when he called. See, Momma wouldn't take me with her when she visited him there. She said it was too dangerous. In fact, she said, they'd had to unlock gates, and all the windows are filled with bars just like the ones in prisons.

"It's funny, he seems like a nice guy," Adam's voice rang from the receiver. "But he killed his parents and grandfather."

"No!" I worried now. "Will they let you keep your sword under your bed?"

"No—no weapons here. In fact, we can't even have fingernail clippers."

"So what if this guy wakes up in the middle of the night and has some kinda flashbacks and goes for you? How can you protect yourself?"

"Don't worry, Li'l Sis, the guards check on us about every hour. So someone will catch him if he tries anything. Besides, what's my specialty?"

"Oh yeah—your Tae Kwon Do." Suddenly, I felt better 'cause I knew Adam's legs could be stronger weapons than Billy clubs. Just the same, I missed Adam, and I was so sorry he went to that place. It seemed more like a prison than a hospital.

Momma went to visit him during the week on a

day she didn't have class. She took Grandma with her, too. I don't know why, 'cause I don't see how when Grandma isn't even five feet tall, and I don't think she could keep a pigeon in line, let alone a mugger. Well, Momma left there in time to pick me up from school.

When I asked her how Adam was doing, she said, "Better," but she didn't tell me much else. Then, when we returned home, she was quiet and the corners of her eyes and lips turned down, all sorrowful like, and right away, she started thumbing through old photo albums. They were really old albums from the days before I was born. One of them contained pictures of Adam when he was a baby, and only went up until he was four or so. Sometimes I liked to look at them myself, to see how dorky he looked. One of them was a picture of him after he'd smashed a banana and wiped it across the tray on his high chair. He still wore diapers then, and his hair was thin. He had a goofy look, too, with his mouth shaped into a tiny "O." You could see bits of banana around his mouth and smeared across his cheeks. The picture made me laugh every time I saw it.

Missouri Western kept Adam there only a week, after the psychiatrist diagnosed him with "being merely histrionic." So either the people there thought it was safe for him to come home or they just got bored with him because he'd killed only a dog and not his parents, girlfriend, or something more interesting. After he returned home, Adam would just shake his head and say the doctors there "didn't know anything."

But Momma had a different take on the matter, which she shared with me, not Adam, one Saturday when he was working at The Haven. We were washing and drying dishes when I asked whether Adam was crazy.

"Haven't you noticed that Adam's calmer now? And yet, he doesn't seem so depressed?" She held one of her ceramic plates under running water, then carefully placed it into the drainer. I didn't like drying those plates because they were so heavy. Besides, my aunt had made them, so if I broke one, Momma would explode, I knew it.

"Yeah. He doesn't cry very often any more." I

eyed the plate and picked it up with both hands. "At least, I haven't seen him. But he says the doctors weren't any good there."

Momma smiled in a weird way: Her eyes looked sad, but the ends of her lips curled upwards. "You know, when Adam lived with his dad, he sent him to an expensive psychiatric institute in Alexandria, where many senators' kids go. And Adam learned all the jargon, all the right words to say to shrinks."

"So?" I couldn't see what she was getting at or why we needed all the history.

"This doctor was onto that. And because Missouri Western doesn't make money off of patients like Adam, the psychiatrists there don't 'overly-diagnose' patients so they can make thousands off of therapy and medications the way doctors for rich people sometimes do. And you see the result, right?"

"I'm not sure I see what you mean."

"Well, Adam kept thinking he was psychotic because some idiot shrink around Washington DC told him he had 'psychotic episodes.' Have you seen him have any such episodes recently?" She smiled.

I shook my head. I figured Adam didn't get any more psychotic than most people I knew. And he certainly wasn't as nuts as Mick.

Momma went on. "Mainly, the problem was his dad and his wife couldn't handle Adam because they spent more time climbing the social ladder instead of paying attention to him—instead of listening to him. I admit, Adam's been tough to handle since he was a baby. But that doesn't mean he's crazy. He just needs more attention than most people. And he hasn't pulled the antics he did with them once he moved here."

"Like what?"

"I heard for some reason, he broke a hole through their bedroom wall."

"He told me about that. He wanted to get some of his antique coins that his dad kept hidden in there. He was afraid his dad would cash them in and not tell him. Plus, his dad always locked the door, even when they weren't home and no one was in the room. So Adam was going to burglarize them—only it was his own stuff he was going to steal. So he made a little bomb with some baking soda and stuff and blew the hole so he could crawl through it. But the hole wasn't nearly big enough."

Momma sighed. "Shoot. You almost can't blame him." Then she glared at me. "But let's not try that around here. I can't afford the repairs."

I shrugged. "You don't need to worry. You never lock your bedroom door."

Then I finished drying the last dish, and hurried up to my bedroom. It was Saturday, so Oprah wasn't on TV, but I wanted to catch some re-runs of *The Simpsons*. And sometimes, on Saturday nights, PBS holds concerts when the station begs people for money. I've gotten to see some good rock groups that way. Nowadays, I like concerts that bring back musicians from the past, especially from the seventies. I like to wear tie-dyed shirts and blue jeans with embroidery on them just like the teenagers did then. Or maybe they did that in the sixties, I'm not sure. On the *Seventies Show*, kids dressed that way, though, so maybe I'm right. Or maybe no one remembers anymore. I heard some comedian say that if you remembered the sixties, you weren't alive then. This didn't make much sense to me. Even if those Hippies did all those drugs, they should still remember the parties, right?

Later that night, something else weird came on *The Channel Nine News*. You see, usually when the news comes on, I flick the station, but this item really caught me: Some guy in Lawrence, Kansas received a mailbox bomb, or at least, someone thought he got one. The TV screen just showed a red, white and blue mailbox. Now, *that's* crazy, crazier than me when I carved on my ankle. And even if Adam was in the psycho ward, I knew he wouldn't do something like that, even if he might *imagine* doing that to someone he hated. Even then, he'd probably only make a little one that wouldn't harm a person much, like the one he used to try to break into his dad's bedroom to rescue his coins.

After Momma and I talked about Adam, I started paying more attention to his moods. It seems she was right: Adam no longer acted so hyper, and yet, he didn't get so down in the dumps, either. Finally, he quit calling

Allie, too, and he even started dating a pretty girl, Sarah, another one he'd met at Longview. She smiled at me a lot, so of course, I liked her immediately. And I especially liked her because she never stuck her nose in the air when she talked to me—or to anyone else.

I wondered, too, if maybe it was okay that I didn't have Adam's wonderful talent with music—it may have made him hypersensitive. Maybe I was better not being so creative. Momma said I'd make a good literature teacher because I liked to read so much. But then, that wouldn't pay much money. Maybe I'd become a lawyer—even if it was too much work. Or maybe an actress. I sure enjoyed performing at the law school review.

Chapter Twenty-Five
Mick Moves On

Mick looked long and hard at The Haven as he sat in his Ford Escort before he took off. Shaped like a giant hamburger, with wide, dark brown stripes down its sides as if they designated the layer of hamburger, the building's orange and blue design would likely forever be imprinted on his brain, along with his army memories. Even inside the car, he could smell French fries. But the smell was likely coming from his clothes—for nine years, he'd smelled like somebody's fast food lunch. Yes, he'd hung in there nine years—nine years of wiping up counters, flipping burgers, dipping fries, and flouring chicken, nine years of covering for people who called in, nine years of scheduling people who often just didn't want to work. Nine years of working eighty-hour weeks, of often giving up holidays and weekends, even after he became a general manager on a Monday-through-Friday schedule.

Finally, after an eternity of wanting to, he'd done it. He'd finally moved up into the real retail world—not just fast-food restaurants. About six months before, Danny Price, one of the former district managers from Hamburger Haven's corporate offices had become a district manager for a huge drugstore chain. And he'd remembered Mick and what a "cracker jack" manager he'd been. Or so Dan said he'd told the upper management. And in two weeks, Mick was to start as general manager for the store at 119th and Metcalf. He'd given notice to The Haven today. No doubt the bigwigs were scrambling to find his replacement, but Mick didn't care. He figured he owed them two weeks notice, no more. In fact, he felt that maybe they owed him. Of course, he'd receive no retirement package. Even if he'd stayed there thirty years, he wouldn't get one. Only the

CEOs and upper management got those. Still, yeah, The Haven owed him. After all, the company had taken nine years of his life, and what did he receive in return? A paycheck, yes, and benefits, which was more than many firms gave anymore. But he had no pension plan. The most The Haven offered was a 401K, and Mick wasn't sure he trusted it. Too many people had lost their shirts in 401K's after the Enron scam.

Suddenly, the lights on the sign went on, as they'd been timed to do at twilight. The evening crew bustled to prepare for the dinner rush, which was seldom as heavy as breakfast and lunch. Adam worked in the back now. He wasn't a bad cook. He was fast and generally, accurate. Mick pulled out a cigarette and lit it. He chuckled. It was ironic that he left The Haven before Adam did.

Maybe the home life would be better now, too. At least, the drug store didn't stay open until midnight and one. So no one would be calling him about a crisis in the wee hours. Maybe now, he and Judith could have a life— if only that Krystal would behave. He worried that it could also be too late, that his days with Judith might be as numbered as his days with The Haven.

It seemed, though, that Adam liked him. Yes, Adam and Rod would have to carry on here. He was glad Adam had returned home, too. Now Mick wasn't outnumbered by females and all their peculiar whims and tantrums. Now, someone could sit with him in the basement and just shoot the breeze while he built furniture and had a beer or two. Now, he had a friend to talk to about this crazy world. Of course, once he started working at the drug store, maybe the world wouldn't seem quite as crazy. At least, he wouldn't come home every night smelling of French fries.

He turned on the ignition and listened for the engine. Yes, it was in time. Now, he could relax—go home and down a couple of beers. It'd been another long day, and he was ready.

Suddenly, the back door of The Haven flew open, and someone came running outside. It was Adam. He scurried down the huge terrace. With Adam's oversized slacks, Mick thought he looked like a goose flapping its wings as he came down to Mick's car. He ran down the slope and arrived panting. "Sorry, but it's important."

Mick cracked his window. "What's wrong?"

"Rod called." Adam looked at Mick and frowned. "He can't make his shift tonight. He just got word today he's being deployed to Iraq. And his dad wants to see him before he ships out. So Rod's booked a plane to Oklahoma City. He said he tried to get one for tomorrow, but they were all booked. So he has to take off tonight. He said he's really sorry and wants you to call him on his cell phone."

"Have you called George?"

"Not home." Adam shrugged. "Maybe you could try Carla."

Mick shook his head. "Our deal was she only works days. That way she can spend evenings with her kids." Mick sighed and rolled up the window. "Shit," he said, then disembarked from the Escort and trudged his way up the long, grassy terrace leading to the brightly lit building that continuously emitted smells of hamburgers and French fries.